A love that won't die...

"I'm here." My words fell from my lips in a hoarse, broken whisper. "I don't know if you can hear me...I wish you could give me some sort of sign." I gently squeezed his hand again, hoping he'd squeeze back if only just a little, but his fingers stayed lax. Loose. Lifeless.

Shit. I couldn't think that way.

"Listen," I said, leaning closer, speaking louder. "I don't know why you came back without telling me. Or why you thought you needed to do this on your own, but you're not alone. Not anymore. You and me, we're together in this and in everything. Okay? I know you're used to taking care of everyone in your life, but this time...*I've got you, Dare.*"

The Brothers Wilde Serials

The Untamed Series:

Untamed

Out of Control

Escaped Artist

Wild at Heart

Rebel Roused

Novels by Jen Meyers

Anywhere

The Intangible Series

Intangible

Imaginable

Indomitable (an *Intangible* novella)

Novels by Victoria Green

Silver Heart

untamed

episode 4: wild at heart

jen meyers & victoria green

wild
at
heart

one
Reagan

They don't know if he'll make it.

Dalia's words rang in my ears, echoing through my head, paralyzing me as people bustled all around the busy Paris airport. My body had frozen; I was unable to move, unable to feel, unable to think. I could see other people's lips moving, but could hear no sounds.

All that existed in this moment was Dalia. And her news about Dare.

"What is he doing in New York?" My phone was pressed hard against my ear. "I thought he was still in Amsterdam. When did that even happen?"

"Oh, god. He didn't tell you?" Dalia said. "Shit, Ree. I'm sorry. Our dad is out and he—"

"*What?!* Your dad is OUT?"

Chills prickled my skin, and I could feel the blood drain from my face. If their father had been released, it could only mean one thing.

My father had done it.

I was almost too afraid to ask, but I had to know. "Dalia…what happened?"

"Dad put Rex in the hospital two weeks ago. Dare went after him."

I closed my eyes, hot tears stinging. *Two weeks ago?* Dare had been in the States for two weeks and hadn't told me?

And it was all because of my fucking father.

"Okay. I'm coming. I'll be on the first flight." I took a deep, shaky breath. "And Dalia?"

"Yeah?"

"Tell him I'm on my way. Tell him to…" I choked back a sob, forcing my voice to be steady. "Tell him to wait for me, okay?"

"I will, Ree," she said. "I will."

I was sprinting for the counter before I even hung up. But the surly ticket agent informed me that I'd just missed the last available seat on the next flight to New York. Not that I could afford the three-thousand-dollar ticket. Hell, I couldn't even afford to travel with luggage at this point. I'd been paying Dare's rent since I'd gotten here, and I didn't have enough left for a last-minute flight home. Not even close.

Since I'd cut myself off from my old lifestyle, I had no credit cards. They were all linked to my parents, anyway, and I knew my mother and father would rather see me suffer than lift a finger to help me. There was no fucking way I'd call them. They would never pay for my ticket—not for it to take me back to Dare—but even if they did, the price they'd extract in return would be much too high.

I tried to think of anyone that I could call. To say that I was lacking in the friend department was an understatement. Dare's family—though the closest thing I had to siblings—were out of the question. And I couldn't possibly ask Sabine for another favor. Especially not when I was on the verge of abandoning her again, after everything she'd done for me. Not that she wouldn't understand, but it was too much. I couldn't impose.

That really left only one person.

And I hadn't talked to him in months. Not since he'd taken my hand and gotten down on one knee. We'd never gone this long without talking. Archer had been my best friend since Crestridge. And, at times, he'd been my only ally.

Now, I had to hope he would be again.

My finger hovered over his name for a moment, and then pressed *Call*. I couldn't afford to hesitate. I didn't know how many moments Dare had left.

As the phone rang, I calculated what time it was in New York, trying to figure out where Archer would be. Knowing him, at nine in the evening, he was already sweet-talking some hot girl into his bed.

I squeezed my eyes shut and pleaded with him to pick up.

Three rings in, I was pretty sure he'd hit *Ignore*, and I started to hyperventilate. Panic filled my lungs.

"Baby girl!" His voice rang out, and I started to cry. "I was wondering how long it would take you to come to your senses. I accept your apolo—"

"Arch?"

He paused and I could almost *hear* the raised eyebrow on the other end of the line. "What's wrong, Reagan? Are you okay? If he did anything to you, I swear I'll—"

"No," I said. "I'm okay. That's not—" My throat closed as I imagined Dare lying in a hospital bed three thousand miles away. And I had to ask Archer, of all people, to help get me to the love of my life. I could barely believe what I was about to say. "It's Dare. He's in New York, and I can't afford the ticket…"

"He left you? He abandoned you in Europe? Reagan," Archer said, and I could picture him pacing as he ran his hands through his wavy, blond hair. "Seriously, babe. You deserve better than—"

"*Archer.*" My voice sounded hoarse. "He's in the hospital. In intensive care." A sob shook me as I pressed my hand to my mouth, fighting to keep my terror contained. I could not fall apart. Not now. Not when Dare needed me to be strong. "Please, Archer. I love him. You were the first person I called. I can't ask my parents for help, you know that. But I need to get to him. And I...I'm *begging* you, Arch. You know what that means."

"Jesus, Reagan." He blew out a ragged breath. "Where are you?"

"Paris."

"Okay. Give me a minute." His voice was muffled as he talked to someone on his end, and I gripped my phone tighter to my ear, my hands cold, my knuckles bone-white. I couldn't relax, not until I had a ticket in my hand.

Every minute...every second—*oh, god.*

"Reagan?" Archer said. "The flights are booked solid. There's nothing for six hours. I'll make the arrangements for you."

"I'm already here. I came to pick him up, but he didn't..." I swallowed. "Which airline?"

"I'm working on it. Go home and pack. Try to relax. Be at Charles De Gaulle at ten. And don't worry about anything...I'll pick you up."

"Really?" A lump formed in my throat. Archer had never picked anyone up from the airport in his entire life.

"It's you," he said softly. "Of course I'll be there." And before I could thank him he said, "Now go. Don't worry. I'll get you home."

When I got back to the airport—bag packed and nerves shot—I realized Archer hadn't told me which airline counter to pick up my ticket from. I was pulling out my phone when it rang.

"AirFrance," he said, not even bothering with a hello.

"Thank you—I was just about to call."

"I know." The warm familiarity of his voice soothed me just a little. Made me feel like I wasn't so alone. I needed that if I was going to make it to New York with eight more hours of uncertainty.

Hurrying for AirFrance, I said, "What time does the flight leave?"

And that's when I saw him. Leaning against the counter underneath the blue-and-white sign, his designer clothes slightly wrinkled. His ice blue gaze filled with concern as I stopped short, mouth hanging open, trying to blink back tears that would not be held back. They rolled down my face as he walked toward me, his hands already reaching for my bag.

"What…?" I couldn't even form a sentence.

"I told you I'd pick you up," he said, raising one eyebrow. "What did you think I meant?"

A laugh sputtered in my throat even as I started to cry, amazed at his gesture, relieved that I wasn't alone. So fucking grateful that he was still my friend.

Archer folded me into his arms. "It's okay, I'm here," he said, holding me tight. "From the sound of your voice, I thought you might need someone with you, that's all."

I nodded into his shoulder and sniffled, not giving a damn that I was a total mess. Today, out of all days in my twenty-two years of life, I was allowed to cry. Just for a little while, because in mere hours…I'd have to be a rock.

No matter what.

"I don't know how to thank you," I said. "I'm so sorry about everything. I just—"

"No," Archer said, leaning his head on mine. "I'm sorry. I never should have pushed the engagement. Pushed us. Especially since I knew how you felt about him. It was a jackass move on my part."

I pulled away and wiped my cheeks with the back of my hand. "Yeah, it was."

He laughed. "Let me make up for it." Grabbing my bag, he waved an arm toward the departure gates. "Your private sky chariot awaits, Lady McKinley. Sushi and copious amounts of bubbly. Unreleased movies. Unrestricted party favors…"

While I appreciated Archer catering to my previous whims, I tuned out the long list of in-flight luxuries.

As long as I had a way to Dare, I couldn't care less how I got there.

two
Reagan

An hour later, Archer and I were ensconced in the over-padded black leather seats of his father's company jet, heading west over the Atlantic. I stared out the window, unseeing, exhausted, overwhelmed.

What if Dare was dying right now? I pulled out my phone to check messages for the thousandth time. What if he was gone before I got there? Before I could see him one more time? Before I could tell him how much I loved him, how much I needed him to fight to stay alive, to fight for me, for us?

My mind was full of what-ifs and questions that no one could answer. Why hadn't he told me his father was out? Or that he was going back to the States? I knew he was protecting me, but I was guilt-ridden over not knowing, angry that he'd failed to tell me. And now he was lying unconscious in a hospital and there was nothing I could do to help.

If he died, I was going to fucking kill him.

God. How could I be angry at him?

"You look like you could use one of these." Archer held out a shot glass filled with something clear and dangerous.

I stared at it, my mouth salivating at the sight, my mind itching for the numbness it guaranteed.

I slid my shaking hands under my thighs and forced out a slow, but steady "No, thanks."

His eyebrows disappeared beneath the hair falling across his forehead. "You okay?"

"Not even close."

"What can I do?" he said.

"You're doing it." I forced a smile. "You've gone above and beyond. I don't know why I was surprised you came to get me. That's been your M.O. forever."

"For you, always."

"Archer…I…" What? What was I going to say to that? He'd flown across the ocean to pick me up in his father's private jet. How could I hurt him again?

"I know, Reagan. It's okay. I'm over it." He shrugged. "I won't say my ego didn't take a beating, but you've always been my favorite. That hasn't changed. I'd still do anything to help you."

"And I, you." Because I would. Archer and I had been through so much together, and he'd always come through for me. I would do the same for him in a heartbeat.

"I know. Now let's go see your brooding artist."

He reached over and squeezed my hand, and I held on tight to him. I'd never been so scared in my life as I was right then, so unsure of what I'd find when I got to the hospital. All I could do at that moment was cling to hope.

It was almost midnight when Archer dropped me off at the hospital. He'd tried to insist on coming up with me, but I'd sent him home. He'd done enough—much more than enough—and this was something I needed to do on my own.

I took the elevator up to the ICU, and quietly passed through the heavy double doors. The smell of sickness permeated the air, and the constant beep and whoosh of machines hooked to patients was all I could hear as I tread silently down the well-lit hall. A nurse looked up in surprise as I rounded the corner, searching for the room Dalia had said Dare was in.

"I'm sorry, Miss," the nurse said with a curt headshake, "but visiting hours are over. You're going to have to come back tomorrow." Her voice was not unkind, but it was firm.

Her words mingled with the noises of machines as I spotted Dare's room. And Dare. There was a wall of windows separating him from the hallway, and although the inside was dim, there was enough light filtering in from the hallway for me to see him lying in the bed, unmoving.

My vision blurred as I took a few steps toward him.

"Miss? You can't be in here…" The nurse got up and headed around the counter to stop me, but I barely noticed.

All I could do was stare at Dare.

My heart pounded, and my breathing faltered. I blinked back tears as quickly as they came, but couldn't stop them.

He wasn't moving. His body was so still, almost as if he—

"Miss!" The nurse blocked my path, her large body eclipsing my view. She had dark brown skin, and warm eyes. Her stern expression filled with empathy as she said, "You can come back during regular visiting hours."

"Is he…" My throat closed and I had to fight to get any sound through. "Is he…dying?"

The word sent a chill down my spine, shivering my already frozen body. My heart felt like it wasn't working at all.

"I'm not allowed to give out patient information." She lowered her voice and leaned closer. "But if he's in this unit, he's still hanging on."

"Please," I said, searching her face through a veil of tears. "I just need to see him for a moment. I flew in from Paris, came straight from the airport...*please*. I can't...I need—"

"*Ree?*"

I looked over the nurse's shoulder at a man standing in the doorway to Dare's room.

"Are you Ree?" he asked. About sixty years old, he had red-rimmed green eyes, long, gray hair pulled back into a pony tail, and a scruffy goatee. He wore a wrinkled, black, button-down shirt over paint-splattered khaki pants. A sling cradled his left arm, and I could see a cast enveloping it.

I nodded at him, wary. He didn't look like anything like Dare—not that I could imagine Dare's father sitting by his bedside after having put him in the hospital in the first place, but you *never* knew with some people. My mother had been at my bedside seven years ago, when she'd been the reason I was there.

Although the guy couldn't be Dare's dad, there was something vaguely familiar about him.

The man tipped his head at the nurse. "She's okay," he said. "She can stay." Then he held a hand out to me. "I'm a friend of the family—Rex Vogel. I've heard a lot about you."

Under normal circumstances I would have fangirled to be in the presence of *the* Rex Vogel, reclusive genius artist that practically NO ONE ever got to meet. Sure, he'd taken Dare under his wing, but that was an anomaly. While Rex's reputation had grown in renown over the years, he'd personally stayed out of the limelight. I'd followed his work for years, but had never even gotten close to meeting him, regardless of how deep my father's pockets had been.

And he was now gently grasping my hand, and pulling me into Dare's room.

As soon as I stepped inside, I lost all thoughts of Rex.

There was only Dare.

He lay so, so still in the bed, bandages covering far too much of his body, bruises blooming over the rest. His right hand was heavily wrapped, and deep red scrapes ran across his handsome face. He looked like he'd lost a fight with a mountain lion. He was connected to so many tubes and machines, and for the first time since I'd known him he seemed completely vulnerable.

I was almost afraid to touch him, but the draw of his presence was too much for me to resist. I was at his side, reaching and hesitating all at once, broken over seeing him like this, but so thankful that he was alive.

"Go ahead," Rex said, quietly. "Touch him. He may be able to feel you, hear your voice. They don't know whether he can hear us, but they've been telling us to talk to him, play music, read out loud. Anything to help bring him back to us." His eyes got redder, and he lay his hand on Dare's shin and squeezed. "You're coming back to us, Dare. You hear me? I won't take no for an answer. Ree is here now. You've at least got to come back for her." Then Rex nodded at me. "I'll leave you alone for a few minutes. Gonna go stretch my legs before I lay down in that chair in the corner. I'm on night duty." He raised one eyebrow. "You staying?"

Nothing could drag me away now that I was finally here.

I nodded. "If that's okay." I looked around the room. There was only the one reclining chair. "I'll sleep on the floor if I have to."

But Rex shook his head. "I'll have them bring in another chair. In fact, I'll go ask the nurse right now." He walked toward the door, then turned to look at me one last time before he left. "I'm glad you're here, Ree. He needs you. He needs us all."

I watched Rex amble out to the nurses' station, then I turned back to Dare.

God. He looked...*broken*.

Ever so gingerly, I ran my fingers down his left arm, careful to avoid the IV line taped there, then slid them into his open hand. It killed me that his fingers didn't automatically wrap around mine.

He couldn't hold my hand right now, but at least I could hold his.

I squeezed his fingers, then leaned down and kissed the one spot on his head that didn't have any cuts or bruises.

"I'm here." My words fell from my lips in a hoarse, broken whisper as my eyes overflowed again. "I don't know if you can hear me…I wish you could give me some sort of sign." I gently squeezed his hand again, hoping he'd squeeze back if only just a little, but his fingers stayed lax. Loose. Lifeless.

Shit. I couldn't think that way.

"Listen," I said, leaning closer, speaking louder. "I don't know why you came back without telling me. Or why you thought you needed to do this on your own, but you're not alone. Not anymore. You and me, we're together in this and in everything. Okay? I know you're used to taking care of everyone in your life, but this time…*I've got you, Dare.* You don't have to worry about anything but getting better." A sob rose in my throat. "Because you've got to come back. Please. I need you. And I love you more than I've ever loved anyone else in my whole life."

Placing a hand on his chest, I felt his heart beat. His pulse had increased when I'd started talking— I'd seen the numbers go up on the monitor to the left of his bed. Did that mean he'd heard me? I could only hope.

"You are mine, Dare Wilde. I own you. Don't

you forget that," I whispered. "You need to be okay because I'm not ready to let you go."

The steady thumping of his heart felt reassuring, even though I knew nothing was sure at this point. But he had to make it through this. He *had* to. There wasn't any other option…because I knew I could not survive losing him.

Not now.

Not ever.

three
Reagan

Over the next week, the hospital became my life. I ate, breathed, and slept by Dare's bedside. The sharp, sterile scent of antiseptic and uncertainty that wafted through the building's white corridors seeped into my pores. No matter how many showers I took, it clung to me like a second skin.

The *beep*, *beep*, *beep* of the heart monitor was a constant in my mind. Even when Dash pried me away long enough to take a shower and change my clothes at his hotel suite, or to just get a breath of fresh air, the sound of Dare's heart echoed within me.

The morning after I'd arrived, I'd woken to Dare's whole family surrounding me—Dalia, Dax, Dash, and his mom Celia. I sat bolt upright at the sight of them, my heart racing, my eyes seeking out Dare in a panic before my ears registered that his heart was still beating.

Thank god. I pressed a hand to my pounding chest.

"Whoa," Dash said, putting a warm, reassuring hand on my shoulder. "Slow down, Ree. Everything's fine."

"*Ish*," Dalia said. "Everything's fine-ish."

Dax flopped down in a straight-backed chair. "Nothing about this is fine-ish. Not even close."

Celia smoothed Dax's hair, her hazel eyes glued to Dare's still form. "No, it's not," she said softly as her eyes started to redden. "But Dare's strong. We've got to keep hoping…your dad couldn't have—"

"Couldn't have what, Mom?" Dax said, his voice filled with anger. "Killed Dare?" He shook his head in disgust. "Sure looks like he tried."

"Dax!" Dalia shot her brother a stern look as she walked up to her mom, wrapping an arm around her thin shoulders and guiding her over to sit in the chair next to Dare's bed.

"Well, it does!" Dax waved his hand at Dare. "Look at what that bastard did to him. I'm just calling it like it is."

Dash gently smacked the back of Dax's head, then gripped his shoulder. "Cool it, man. We all know what happened, and this is hard on *everyone*—especially your mom. No point making it any harder."

Dax shook off Dash's hand, mumbled something I couldn't quite make out as he glared sullenly from his chair.

"You're his Ree?" Celia was looking at me, her head tilted to one side, her long, dark waves tucked behind her ears. I nodded. "He's told me so much about you. I'm glad you're here."

"Me, too." Glancing around the room again, I realized Rex was gone. "Where's Rex?"

"He went home for a few hours. He'll be back." Celia reached out and squeezed Dare's arm. "He's spent almost every minute here since they found Dare…" Her eyes watered as she pressed a hand to her mouth.

I felt wildly uncomfortable, so I padded out into the hall to give them a little time to themselves. I walked past the nurses' station, not having any actual clue where to go, feeling lost and overwhelmed. And when Dash quietly called my name a few moments later, relief washed over me.

He took one look at my face, opened his arms, wrapped them around me, and I hugged him tight, letting myself lose it.

"I know," he said. "It's unbearable to see him like that."

I nodded into his chest, unable to speak.

"He'll come back to us, Ree. I have to believe he will. I can't lose my brother—not having only just found him." He choked on those last words and tightened his arms around me. "We all have to hang in there, give him time to heal."

"Dash, what happened?"

"We don't really know. He went after our dad and was found the next day nearly beaten to death." He shook his head, his whole body tensing as he slowly released me and ran a hand through his shaggy hair. "He was unconscious, had multiple broken ribs, and his right hand…" He closed his eyes as if he were in pain.

"What?" I said. "What's wrong with his hand?"

"It was crushed. Broken bones, severed tendons." His jaw tightened. "Like Dad wanted to make sure Dare wouldn't ever be able to use it again."

My breath flew out of me like I'd been kicked in the gut. Dare was right-handed. If that hand was severely damaged…

Jesus.

I just…there was nothing to say to that.

Dash showed me around the ICU, so I knew where everything was, and then we went back to Dare's room to hope. And wait.

And wait.

And wait.

Now, a week later, I still sat by Dare's side. *Always by his side.*

I could barely eat, but at least once a day I forced down a few bites of soggy salad from the cafeteria just so I could function on some basic level. I even drank the nasty coffee from the vending machine. If only to stay awake. In case…

"Wake up," I whispered over his soft, ragged breathing. "Please, Dare."

The alternative was too painful to bear.

"Please, please, *please*. Open your eyes, baby. Come back to me." I brought my lips to his ear, but didn't risk touching him. There were too many cuts and bruises, too many bandages on his head. And his right hand—the one with the bandages and splint—constricted my heart and knotted my stomach every time I looked at it.

The doctor said surgery had repaired the damage, but they didn't know how much use he would regain until it healed. Whether he'd be able to paint. Or draw. Or tattoo. All of the things he loved most in this world.

Not that it mattered right now. Nothing mattered except him waking up.

I looked around the room at the people stuck in this godforsaken limbo with me. Dalia had finally drifted off to sleep, her tall, lean frame contorted in the chair. Dax sat across from me, bouncing his knees and typing away on his cell, all the while cursing their father under his breath.

Rex was motionless by the widow, staring out onto the busy street, lost in his own thoughts. He hadn't said much over the past seven days, but the turbulent expression in his eyes revealed a war waging beneath the surface of his stony silence.

Dash had taken Celia to get something to eat.

The woman was all skin and bones and dark under-eye circles, looking like she wanted nothing more than to be hooked up to Dare's morphine drip. And I couldn't blame her. I, too, was itching for a way out of the anguish suffocating me. Every second of waiting, hoping, fearing the worst was bringing me closer to the point of breaking, but I knew I couldn't turn to pills. No matter what, I had to stay sober and strong for Dare.

Now and always.

Regardless of what the future might have in store for us.

"Ree…" Dare is calling my name, his voice thin and raw. I keep reaching for him, but he slips away, dissolving and disappearing from my grasp.

Over and over again.

I reach and he's gone. I reach and he's gone.

"Dare wait!" I cry.

I can't move fast enough. My arms are too heavy to lift, my feet won't budge.

He calls my name again. "Ree…"

I awoke to an empty, dim room, my chair pulled up next to Dare's bed, my head nestled on the mattress beside him. My braid was a matted blonde mess and my eyes stung.

But something was different. Something *felt*

different.

My pulse began to race faster than the steady beeping of the monitor. I could *feel* someone watching me.

And there was only one other person in the room.

four
Reagan

"Ree…" he said softly, breathing my name like it gave him life. The sound was weak and groggy, but it was Dare's voice.

Dare!

I turned my head to find him looking down at me with familiar chocolate brown eyes—eyes I hadn't seen for weeks. A tsunami of relief washed over me, and I sat up so fast the room swayed.

"DARE!" He flinched, so I dropped my voice to a whisper. "How…when…?" My thoughts were a mere jumble of words I couldn't string together into a coherent sentence. "Oh, god…" I leaned over and gently pressed my hand to his cheek, careful to avoid his shattered cheekbone, unable to stop my tears from bursting forth like a storm.

"What's wrong? Why are you crying, Ree?"

I couldn't help it. I had never been more thankful for anything in my entire life. "You're awake. I feel like my world is right again," I said.

Far from perfect, of course, but at least it was back to rotating on its axis. "I have to get your mom. And Dash, Dalia, and Dax. Rex has been spending all his time here, too. And that doctor...*oh, god*...everyone will be—"

"Doctor?" Confusion clouded his eyes. "Where am I?" He tried to sit up, but his head immediately fell back against the pillow as he groaned in pain. "Jesus. What's going on?" He sounded so lost and disoriented, so unlike himself, which only made me cry harder.

"You're...you've been...oh, god, Dare...you..."

"Ree," he cut me off, wincing as he turned his head to kiss my palm. "Stop. *Breathe.*"

I nodded, my tears slowing, the anguish in my heart giving way to a small light of hope. He was alive. In the end, that was all that truly mattered.

And...he knew who I was.

He tried to raise his hand, but his face contorted in pain. "I've been dying to reach out and touch you, but it fucking kills to move."

"Don't," I said, bringing my face to his. "I'll come to you." I gave him a light peck, the roughness of his cracked lips scraping against my skin. Yet I couldn't help but smile. Even broken, Dare Wilde was the most beautiful man I'd ever seen. And he belonged to me. "I was so afraid you might not remember me."

"Not remember you?" A small smirk tugged at

the corners of his lips. "Time and time again, you've proven impossible to forget."

"I just meant..." Shit. They'd said he could have memory loss due to the severity of the concussion. Yet here he was...bruised, beaten, and bloodied, but still very much *mine*. "I'm so glad you're awake."

"How long have I been here?" He surveyed the room. "In the hospital."

"A little over a week," I said, slipping my hand into his and relishing the fact that his fingers held on tight. "Do you remember..." *Your attack? Your father's attempt at your life? Your near-death experience?* "...what happened?"

"I don't know." Shutting his eyes, he gave a little headshake. "Rex got hurt. And I came back to deal with that. I...I don't remember anything more."

I wasn't sure whether to be relieved or upset that there were things he didn't remember. We'd been told to expect this, that it was common. I almost hoped Dare would have no recollection of the horror his father had put him through. And mine, too.

I kissed him again and stood up. "I have to get your family in here, they've been so worried—"

"No. Stay, Ree." He didn't release my hand. "I want a moment alone with you. Just to...*be*."

"HOLY CRAP!" Dalia yelled from the

doorway, startling us both. "DARE!"

I cringed at the volume of her voice, but smiled at Dare.

"Do you know who that loud shriek belongs to?" I whispered before turning my attention to his sister who was already flying across the room.

"Terror One," he said as she beamed down at him from the other side of the bed.

"It's about time you woke up. You ready to rumble or what?" Dax nudged his sister out of the way. "I know I can take you right now, because, honestly, you look like shit."

Dalia elbowed him in the stomach, doubling him over in pain.

"Take it down a notch or two." Dash walked around them, sending me a look of pure, raw relief. "You had us worried there for a while."

Then Celia was rushing into the room, and they were all stepping aside so she could get to Dare. I tried to give them a moment, but Dare wouldn't let go of my hand. As I began to gently ease my fingers out of his grasp, he tightened his grip and shot me a smile, telling me that I was a part of them all. That I was family.

And my heart nearly burst with love and relief.

This previously somber room was suddenly filled with celebration and laughter. Of course, we weren't out of the woods yet. There was so much more healing he had to do, and we wouldn't know the outcome of his injuries for a while, but we'd been so desperate for a single moment of reprieve, a tiny drop of happiness, that none of us cared.

Dare tired out pretty quickly, so when he fell asleep again, I took the opportunity to get out of the ICU and simply move around.

I was totally wired—high on Dare's first step to recovery, and high on life again. I *knew* he'd get through this. And I *knew* he'd be okay. Deep down, I just knew everything was going to work out. I could feel it.

And that realization made me want to skip down the hallways and sing at the top of my lungs. But since I was in the ICU, surrounded by people still waiting for good news—or any news at all—I opted instead to make the next coffee run.

"I've got this," I said, when Dash offered to come along. "That vending machine and I are now practically BFFs."

I made it halfway to the lounge on the other side of the wing before my buzz was killed by the appearance of the one person I'd been dreading meeting since I'd left for Paris all those months ago.

My father.

five
Reagan

"*Reagan.*"

If looks could kill, both of us would be on our way to the morgue right now.

"What the hell are you doing here?" I asked through gritted teeth, my hands fisted at my sides. It was taking every ounce of self-control to keep my voice steady. "No, wait. A better question is: what the hell did you do?" I motioned in the direction of Dare's room.

"I am glad to see that you have finally come to your senses and returned home," he said coolly. "Although, I do not appreciate being addressed in such a tone or with such language."

Was he fucking kidding me?

"How could you let that animal out of prison?"

My father shook his head and sighed. "I see some things have not changed. You are still as hysterical as always. I do not have the slightest idea what you are talking about, Reagan."

"I'm talking about a murderer and a drug lord who is now running free on your streets, *Mayor* McKinley."

"Keep your voice down." He took a step forward and grabbed my shoulders, towering above me. "*Now.*"

"Let me go or I'll scream." I bit off each word. "NOW."

A couple of nurses had stopped in the hallway and were eyeing us.

"Mayor!" The older one gushed. "What an honor!"

"The pleasure is all mine, ma'am" he said in that smooth political drawl he always used when talking to The People. "I am just visiting my youngest daughter who's volunteering while on sabbatical from Harvard."

Motherfucker.

"Oh?" The nurse's silver eyebrows rose as she turned to me. "How nice of you, dear."

"I suppose," I said, matching my father's fake smile. "If you call seeing my *boyfriend* volunteering."

The younger nurse seemed to perk up at the mention of a guy. "Oh, does he work here? Don't tell me it's Doctor Rivers!"

I shook my head. "He's a patient. Interesting story, actually. He was just—"

"*Excuse us.*" My father took hold of my elbow

with an iron grip, and began to pull me away. "It was lovely to meet you, but we must be on our way." He dragged me around the corner before I was able to finally pull my arm free.

"The volunteer lie was ridiculous enough, but did you really have to throw Harvard in there, too?" I snapped. "Talk about overkill."

"It was no lie," he said. "You will be going to Harvard next semester. I cannot even bear to discuss how much this little European stunt you pulled has cost me. You are twenty-two years old, Reagan. It is time for you to start behaving like an adult."

I scoffed. "You mean 'behaving like a McKinley,' don't you? Because that's who you want me to be, isn't it? Your *perfect* daughter who does everything you want, no questions asked. Well, you already have one of those. Her name is Quincy." I crossed my arms over my chest. "And, sorry to disappoint you, but Quinn and I are nothing alike."

My father flexed his jaw and took a deep breath before responding. "Do not be difficult, Reagan. You are only making this harder on yourself."

"THIS? There is NO *this*! Especially not after what you did to Dare! If you think I'm going to do anything for you then you're out of your fucking mind. I have my own life now. One that doesn't involve the McKinley name. I've already dropped Reagan and I'm strongly considering adopting a new last name. What do you think about Ree Wilde?"

I laughed at my father's outraged expression. Truth be told, I'd never given marriage any thought. Dare and I had only just begun this journey toward a solid, stable relationship. We had a lifetime to contemplate where it was going.

I'd simply said it for shock value. And it clearly worked.

Game, set, and ma—

"That degenerate is going straight to prison."

I laughed again because the man was CLEARLY insane. "For what? Getting almost killed by the convict that you released?"

"The boy has blood on his hands," he said, his face stony. "Two bodies were found at the scene. The police suspect Daren Wilde Sr. but that can be changed with a simple phone call. So if you want your little fling to have a chance at freedom, you will do as I say. I am in the middle of my campaign for governor, and I need the entire family to present a united front."

"You're blackmailing me into playing house?" All laughter was gone. In its place was incredulity. "Do you realize how ridiculous that sounds?"

"You are giving me no choice. I am done tolerating your juvenile games. McKinleys are conquerors—not *quitters*. Time to come home,

Reagan." He reached for me again, but I took a step back.

"It's Ree. And I'm not going anywhere with you." I would NOT let history repeat itself. I was done letting my father control me. "You don't own me anymore," I said coolly. "And there's blood on your hands, too. Do you think your beloved fans would support your run for governor if they knew about all the filthy under-the-table dealings you've been involved in over the years? Not to mention, you're the one who let that monster out of jail. *You* did this. And if you even dream of fucking with Dare, I'll tell everyone what I know." I pushed past him, but he caught my arm.

"You can't prove it," he said, squeezing hard.

I shook my head. "I don't have to. Like you always told me, perception is king. If people *think* you did it, that's all that matters." I glanced down at his hand still gripping my arm. "And if you don't think I'll actually do it...*just try me*. Now let go of my arm."

His eyes narrowed, but he released me, and I ran back to Dare's room.

I paused outside his door, leaning against the wall for a moment to compose myself. Squeezing my eyes shut, I breathed deeply to stop the nausea rising up in me. All the adrenaline that had been coursing through my body during the fight with my father seemed to leave me at once, making my knees weak and my head spin.

Dare was my first thought.

Pills was my second.

Thank god the first one was stronger a thousand times over.

I could do this. I could be brave enough for both of us.

Even if it meant picking a fight with fucking Goliath.

six
Dare

My memory returned in pieces. Unwelcome, fragmented pieces of failure. I'd been stupid enough to go after my father unarmed, unprepared. Why hadn't I anticipated the ambush? My hatred had blinded me and made me forget that I wasn't dealing with a man, but an animal. My fear for my family's safety had forced me to act in haste. But I'd just wanted him gone. Out of our lives once and for all.

I'd had something on him—enough to make him disappear. Of that, I was certain. Except, I couldn't recall a single card I'd been holding that day. It had been a little over a week since I'd woken up, and the whole deck was still strewn all over the place, my ace nowhere in sight. My mind refused to cooperate, and my body was even more useless.

Especially my hand.

"Stop worrying, Dare," my mom said when she

caught me staring at the splint for the hundredth time today. "The doctor said the surgery was a success. You'll be painting again in no time."

She had a permanent smile tattooed on her pale lips. Her eyes, though, were as empty as when she used. Cleary, the fantasy land she was living in had unrealistic happy endings no matter what. But at least she was no longer calling me Daren. She never did after a trip to the hospital. For a while, at least.

"He hasn't tried to contact you, has he?" I hated to ask, and I despised even more that I wasn't sure I'd believe her answer.

She shook her head. "No. And even if he did, I wouldn't..." She pressed her lips together, unable to finish the sentence.

We both knew she would. Because she *had*. Time and time again, she'd allowed him back into our lives. Even when four-year-old Dalia cried and begged her not to "let the scary man come home from the place bad people go to." Even when seven-year-old Dax had suffered a broken arm while trying to be his strung-out mommy's hero.

"You can't let him intimidate you, mom," I said. "You have to be strong this time or we'll never be rid of him. I'll find a way to send him back where he belongs. I promise." I had something on him. I was sure of it. I just needed my fucking brain to catch up and remember *what*.

"You'll find a way to send him to hell?" Dax arched an eyebrow from across the room.

"Hell would be Club Med for that monster," Dalia said with a bitter laugh as she propped her legs up on a chair.

I pointed at the acting book in her hands. "You need to get back to California. Back to work and classes. Back to your own life." Turning my gaze to Dax, I added, "And you're not gonna have another record-setting year if you don't get your ass on the field." His body was constantly in motion, his hands restless for a football the way mine were for a paintbrush.

Dax cracked his knuckles and began pacing around the room. "No way. We're not leaving you. Not with him out to get you. I'm no longer some little kid, Dare. I can help." He fisted his hand and pointed it at me. "I can fight."

"You have school," I said. "There will be no fighting on anyone's part. The police are taking care of things." No one believed that, but it had to be said. There was no way in hell I would let Dax anywhere near our father. The prick fought dirty.

My mind chose this particular moment to mock me with snippets of the attack. Three of my father's goons had jumped me before I even got to him. They'd ensured I was broken and unable to fight back before delivering me, so he could finish the job.

"The police?" Dalia snorted. "Yeah, right. Sure they are. The way they always take care of things when his tainted money is involved."

"Mom?" Dax looked to our mother for help. "We don't have to go back, do we?"

"Well…" Her eyes widened as her gaze flitted between Dax and me. "Maybe they can stay a little longer."

"This isn't some slumber party, Mom. We're dealing with real danger and real responsibility." Something she knew very little about. She'd been high for half of my life. Keeping my siblings on track had always fallen to me—she wasn't qualified to make this call.

"I have to go back to L.A. for a while," Dash said from the doorway. "Take care of some…stuff." He was back to scratching his wren tattoo. If I hadn't done it myself, I'd think the damn thing was infected. "Why don't you guys come back with me?"

"Great. It's settled then." I had no idea when or how my father would strike again. Once I got the twins out of New York, I'd have two less people to worry about as I tried to get my shit together.

I looked up at Ree. She stood next to Dash, a tray with four coffee cups in her hands. A soft smile was painted across her lips.

My heart ached. She'd been taken in by my

family and accepted as one of us. It was like she'd been made not only for me, but for all of us, the way she fit in so easily. And she'd barely left my side since I'd woken up.

She was the light of my days and nights. I needed her with every beat of my heart.

I glanced down at my mangled hand, then back up at Ree again, worry washing over me.

My dad finding out about her scared me shitless...and I had no idea why.

I bite back a groan as he continues to pound on my face. There's a sickening sound of bones shattering, but I'm unable to process the pain. My mind is numb, and my body has gone into shock. At least this way the sadistic prick isn't getting the satisfaction of hearing me suffer.

"You think YOU can threaten ME, you piece of shit?" My father's voice is strained and rough, and though one of my eyes is swollen shut, I can clearly see the veins in his temple and neck bulging. "Did you forget who I am?"

"You're an old fuck," I say through a mouthful of blood. "You were always a cheap fighter, but now you need others to do your dirty work because you can't perform." Those words earn me another hit across the jaw. There is something metal wrapped around his knuckles—a rusty chain that stings like a sonofabitch. I smile despite my busted lip. "That's why you had your men string me up like some captured animal instead of facing me like a

man."

I brace myself for another hit, but it doesn't come. Instead, he releases the bindings and sends me tumbling to the cement floor. Although two of his guys have their guns trained on me, I need to get a hit in before I die. But before I can get to my feet, my father slams something hard over my head, and my face kisses the ground.

"If you're gonna kill me," I shout through ragged breaths, "fucking do it already!" I shut my eyes and picture Ree's face. She was the one who'd gotten me through the past three hours of torture. She's the only thing still keeping me alive.

"Oh, I'm not going to kill you, son. If I was going to do that, you would have been dead hours ago." He bends down to my level and pulls my right hand forward. "No, I'm going to do something much, much worse." Realization hits me hard in the gut before he even raises the two-by-four he's holding. "You took away everything. My freedom. My business. You turned my wife and kids against me. Now I'm going to return the favor." The wood connects with the top of my right hand. HARD. "First, I'll destroy everything you care about." He hits me again and I feel my knuckles shatter. "Slowly." Another hit. "Painfully." Nausea washes over me as I begin to see white spots in front of my eyes. "Piece by fucking piece." My hand is smashed to a bleeding pulp and I'm about to black out.

"You're going to let him live?" one of his henchmen says. "He's seen our faces! What the hell?"

My father turns his head and gives a curt nod. A single

gunshot rings through the air, followed by a silence that's only disturbed by my wheezing and the sound of a body hitting the ground. My ribs are broken, and I almost wish I could feel the pain. Feel fucking something other than terror and dread. But the next words out of my father's mouth confirm my worst fears.

"I'm going to let you live so you can watch me destroy everyone you love."

"NO!" My eyes snapped open. I was alone in my quiet hospital room—the noise of the ICU left behind. Dash, Dalia, and Dax had left days ago, my mom was out getting a bite to eat with Rex, and Ree was supposed to be back any minute.

My heart pounded as the memory filtered into my mind again, and I broke out into a cold sweat.

He was going to hurt everyone, including Ree. *Especially* Ree.

How much did he already know?

"I think my father's people are tailing me." Ree entered the room, shaking off rain from her long, red coat. "Either that, or I'm seeing things," she said as she bent over to kiss me. "What's wrong?" She stopped an inch away from my mouth when she saw my expression. "Oh, god. Does something hurt? Do you want me to call the nurse?"

I slowly shook my head, feeling the blood drain from my face. "What did they look like?"

"The stalkers?" She shrugged. "Like creepy assholes."

"I'm serious, Ree."

"I don't know. Two bulky guys in a dark sedan who've been hanging around my hotel for the past week," she said, frowning. "He's done this before. Many times. He's pissed I haven't run back home and wants to keep tabs on me."

"Maybe." Or maybe it was my father who wanted to prove that he held the whole fucking deck in his hands now. Did he know about Ree? What was he going to do to her?

Shit. His words rang in my mind again. She wasn't safe. I had to get her the fuck out of here and away from me NOW.

"Dare," she was calling my name, her blue eyes wide with fear. "You're scaring me."

"You can't come to the hospital anymore." Every word cut deep into me like a fucking dagger, but I couldn't risk her life.

Her mouth popped open in confusion. "What? What are you talking about?"

"You shouldn't be here," I said.

"Dare…" She gently touched my arm. "Where else would I be?"

Somewhere safe. Away from me. "Ree, you can't—"

"I don't understand." She shook her head. "Did my father threaten you? Is it about the dirt he's got on you? Because I can take care of that, Dare.

He's not going to hurt you. I swear. I'm strong enough to stand up to him this time."

"It's not your father."

"Well, whatever it is, I'm not going anywhere."

Goddamn it. That's what I was afraid of most. "You've gotta leave, Ree."

"You're not making any sense," she said. "Did they change your medication? Because you're sounding paranoid."

I shook my head. "It's not the meds."

"Well, then what the hell is going on, Dare?"

More memories came flooding back. *I loved your mother, you know. And you made her hate me. So now I'm not going to rest until I find the one woman YOU can't live without and tear her apart. While you watch.*

"Is it YOUR father?" She was staring at me, her hands on her hips, her cheeks flushed. She was so fucking amazing, and all I wanted to do was take her in my arms and kiss her until she couldn't tell up from down.

And my father would kill her if he found out.

"Ree, you have to listen to me—"

"NO," she said, her eyes sparking with anger. "You have to listen to me. I love you, and I'm not leaving you. We have been through far too—"

"*I'm trying to save your life,*" I yelled, and her eyes went wide. "My dad will kill you if he finds out about you." His words echoed in my mind, over and over again.

"Dare, come on." She was trying to comfort me, reaching for me, but I flinched away. "You can't really believe—"

"LOOK AT ME, REE." I held up my bandaged hand and waved at the rest of my battered body. "You don't think he'll do worse than this to you? He *told* me he would. As he was beating the shit out of me, he SWORE IT." I wanted to grab her by the shoulders and shake her, get her to understand how fucking serious this was. "You have NO IDEA what we're dealing with, and I…"

My voice caught, and I couldn't get the words out. Her brow was crinkled, her eyes filled with concern. Silently, she reached out for my hand. I held on like she was my fucking lifeline.

When I could finally speak, my voice was thick and raw. "I can't stand the thought of losing you—I'd die if something happened. *Please*," I said. "Please just go."

"For how long?" She spoke quietly, her expression wary and unconvinced.

"I don't know." I shook my head. "Until I can figure out how to make him go away."

"But maybe I can help. Maybe I can—"

"No."

"But I might be able to—"

"NO."

"We're a team, Dare. You don't—"

"No, we're not. Not this time. This is my shit,

and I have to be the one to deal with it."

Her mouth snapped shut and she pressed her lips together. "*Fine.*" She yanked her coat back on, grabbed her bag, then stormed toward the door. It took all of my self-control to not stop her. At the last minute, she turned around and glared at me. "You know, once in a while you could actually accept some help when you really need it, and not be such a stubborn asshole."

Then she was gone.

It felt like all the air was suddenly sucked from the room, like I couldn't breathe, like a piece of me had been ripped from my body.

Rex came in a moment later, just as I hurled an empty tray across the room. He raised his thick gray brows, turning his head and looking down the hall after Ree.

"What was that about? Is Ree okay?"

I shook my head, grinding my teeth together until my jaw hurt. "I sent her away." Fuck. What was this pain in my chest? Either I was having a heart attack at the ripe old age of twenty-five or my fucking heart was breaking.

"Why would you do that?" Rex looked incredulous. He pointed in the direction Ree had fled. "That girl is the love of your life. What are you doing, Dare?"

I told him what I remembered, and his face lost all color.

"Aw, shit." He shook his head.

"Dad won't hesitate hurting her. Hell, he would *kill* her if he knew how much she meant to me." My throat closed at the thought of my father getting hold of Ree and punishing her to get back at me. "I can't risk her life, Rex. I fucking love her." I shoved my hand through my hair, and looked up at him. "Will you do me a favor and look after her? Keep her safe?" Goddamn, my fucking heart hurt even more than my hand. I rubbed my chest as if that would help. "Please, Rex? I need to know she's okay."

He nodded once, then jerked his head toward the hallway. "I better go after her." He pointed at me again. "But we're not done discussing this. You can't do everything on your own, you know. You don't have to. Not when you have someone who loves you as much as that girl does."

Then he was gone.

I hated the thought of sending Ree away more than she could even imagine. She was the biggest part of me. But if I had to so I didn't lose her forever...then the pain was worth it.

I just hoped I could get rid of the bastard. If I stood a chance at destroying him, though, my memory had to return.

Where the fuck was that card? Where the hell was my ace?

seven
Reagan

I made it all the way out to the elevators before falling apart. My chest split in two and I couldn't breathe. I leaned against the wall, pressing my back into it as I stared up at the ceiling, willing myself to keep my shit together.

But my shit quickly shattered.

My knees gave out, and I slid down the wall as sobs shuddered from deep inside me, quivering through me as they spilled out. My butt hit the floor and I tucked my head in between my knees and cried. People walked by without bothering me—I was in a freaking hospital, a place where people got all kinds of bad news. I didn't exactly stand out.

But then Rex's hand lay gently on the back of my head. He didn't say anything, he just sat on the floor next to me and stayed there. Which only made me cry harder.

I couldn't believe this was happening.

Not again. Not like this.

Every time my life finally hit the right track, a huge boulder planted itself right in front of the fucking train and stopped me from moving forward. Over and over again. Sobriety wasn't even my biggest issue anymore. Not when I was so close to losing my damn sanity.

What the hell was Dare doing? I didn't understand why nothing was ever easy with us. I mean, we LOVED each other. We were freaking soulmates.

And, yes, I'd always thought that was a ridiculous notion—*soulmates*—because it sounded like some idiotic, over-romanticized, hearts-and-flowers bullshit.

But I'd been wrong. It was very real, and it was the reason my heart felt like it was being ripped right out of my chest as I sat there sobbing in the hospital hallway.

Rex passed me some tissues once I was all cried out and sniffling.

"I don't get it," I said. "Why is he pushing me away? Why won't he let me help?"

He sighed. "He has his reasons—not that I agree that this is the way to handle things—but he's trying to do the right thing." His voice was kind and brimming with genuine concern.

"How can THIS possibly be right?"

"I don't know what to tell you." Rex shook his

head sadly. "Just…give him time. Okay? If you can, don't give up on him. I realize that's probably asking too much of you right now, but…"

"No, it's fine." I scrambled to my feet, suddenly needing to get out of there. Hurrying over to the elevators, I pushed the down arrow, then turned to him. "Thank you, Rex. I just…I'm gonna go…"

Oh, shit. I had nowhere to go, no one to go to, no job, and I was running out of money fast. I couldn't go to my parents. No. I *wouldn't* go to them. Archer was on a business trip, so I couldn't even crash with him. The city I'd been in love with for most of my life suddenly felt like a cold, uncaring stranger.

Rex noted the uncertainty on my face and said, "Do you not have a place to stay?"

I shook my head, my eyes filling with tears again. "I'm going to look for something first thing tomorrow."

Rex rose to his feet. "There's a little one-bedroom apartment over my studio. It's yours if you'd like it."

"Really?"

"Absolutely. We can go there now, get you settled in."

The elevator dinged, the doors opened, and Rex waved me in ahead of him. Just as they were about to close, Celia came around the corner.

"Rex!" she called, and he put a hand out to stop the doors.

He looked at me. "Give me a second, okay?"

Nodding, I stepped back out of the elevator, and walked over to the windows looking out over the city to give them some privacy. But even though they stood on the other side of the room, I could clearly hear their conversation.

"He's going to be released tomorrow," Celia said. "But we don't have a place for him yet. Can he stay in your apartment?"

Rex paused, then said, "The space is already spoken for. And it wouldn't be safe for him anyway. If Dare's hoping to keep a low profile, he can't be staying with me."

"Oh, god," she said. "I hadn't even thought of that."

"But I might know of a place. A friend of mine is looking for a new tenant. I'll make a call."

Watching their reflections in the window, I saw Celia shake her head. "I can't pay for it," she said. "And Dare has hardly anything left. After all these hospital bills…"

Rex put his hands up, waving her concerns away. "You don't have to worry about it. I'll cover him for now, until he can get back on his feet."

"You know how he is, Rex. He won't let you."

"Well, he doesn't exactly have a choice this time, does he? He can pay me back. I'll see if I can find some art buyers for him in the meantime." Rex shrugged. "We'll work it out, Cee. Let's just get him out of here and settled so he can heal." He glanced over toward me, and I flicked my focus off their reflections, and back on the vista again. "I've got to take Ree home. I'll be back later."

Then Celia was saying goodbye and disappearing down the hall while Rex and I got back into the elevator. As we walked to the hotel to pick up my things, I couldn't stop thinking about their conversation.

And I couldn't keep my mouth shut.

"I can set up a show for Dare at La Période Bleue," I said. "I know Sabine will say yes."

Rex didn't say anything for a moment. "You heard." It wasn't an accusation, just a statement of fact.

"I wasn't trying to eavesdrop. I swear. It just—"

"No, it's fine, Ree. Dare needs all the help he can get, even when he thinks he has to do it all himself. Or maybe especially then." He nodded. "A show would be an incredible help, actually. He told me he has quite a number of works at his studio in Paris. He could sell those." His face was getting more animated the more he thought about it. "Yes. This would be perfect. If you could set it up, I'll present it to Dare." He shot me a worried glance. "I just think it'll be best coming from me right now."

"Yeah," I said. "Of course. He doesn't even have to know that I had anything to do with it. That's fine. Really. I'll stay out of it." I ducked my head, not wanting Rex to see the fresh hurt reflected on my face.

Placing his hand on my arm, he stopped me. "Ree. It's just for the time being. Trust me on this. He'll come around because he'll have to. He can't fight this battle alone, no matter how much he thinks he has to. And having seen the way he looks at you…" He gave me a reassuring smile. "You two belong together."

I tried to take comfort in that, but at the moment, all I wanted to do was curl up in a ball and cry.

Which is exactly what I did about an hour later. We collected the meager amount of stuff I'd brought from Paris, grabbed a cab to Rex's house, and he left me to settle into the apartment while he went back to the hospital. My bags sat exactly where I'd dropped them before I collapsed on the bed.

The more I thought about it, the more I realized that this could all be fixed by my father. He could put Dare's dad back behind bars where he belonged, and then Dare and I would be free to be together. Dare wouldn't have to worry about my safety or anyone else's.

It would solve everything.

Instead of feeling sorry for myself, I got angrier and angrier as I stewed on the fact that none of this would have happened if my father had kept his fucking nose out of my business. That everything that had happened to Dare and his family these past weeks was a direct result of my father's interference.

And I was not going to just sit here and take it. All my life I'd gone along with everything my parents wanted, never rocking the boat, never confronting them.

But that was the old Reagan. The new Ree wasn't going to take their shit anymore, nor tolerate their meddling in my life.

I was going to make sure they knew that once and for all.

Right fucking now.

eight
Reagan

The lobby of my parents' Upper East Side penthouse was bustling with well-dressed New York elite. Two broad-shouldered guards framed a tiny, blonde event planner who was checking names off a list before the guests filed into the elevator. Despite my scowl and lack of party attire she waved me through without hesitation.

Finally, all those photo ops had paid off.

The elevator door opened into the grand foyer—newly redecorated by my mother. I was still trying to gain my bearings when I was ambushed by my sister.

"Goodness, Reagan!" Quinn said as she took in my jeans and oversized blue sweater. "You better change immediately." Looking over her shoulder, she lowered her voice to a whisper. "Some very important members of the press are attending this event."

I let out a low whistle. "If I didn't know any

better, I'd think I was talking to our mother's clone. Oh, wait…"

"You look like trash." She wrinkled her nose as if I also *smelled* like trash. "What has Europe done to you?"

"Woken me up to the crazy that is our family," I said with a laugh. "You should try it sometime."

"It's too late for our dear Quincy," Pierce said as he entered the foyer, a glass of scotch in his hand. "She's already cultivating a Stepford Spawn." He pointed to our sister's swollen stomach. "But I do have to say, Reagan, I'm quite impressed to see that you've finally grown some balls. Wish I could just fly to Europe on a whim and have a fling or two."

"You do that all the time." Quinn sighed dramatically. "Daddy is paying dearly to cover that mess you and your friends made in Bangkok last month."

Pierce grinned. "That? Please, that was just a bunch of cheap wh—"

"No! Stop!" she cried and placed a hand on her bump as if to shield her unborn child's ears.

"Reagan!" My mother's eyes widened when she caught sight of me, her face sporting her usual third-martini-and-second-Xanax flush. She wore a dark blue suit—clearly picked out by some stylist to offset the icy daggers in her pale eyes. Too bad they couldn't do anything about her frosty tone.

"You cannot enter this house wearing such a horrendous ensemble!"

God, I missed Paris. And Amsterdam.

Even rehab had been better than this.

"I've already told her to change." Quinn turned to our mother, smiling proudly.

"Jesus." I groaned. "Are you waiting for a 'good girl' pat and a fucking treat, Quinn?"

Pierce stifled a laugh as my mother gasped. "Be civil, Reagan." She nervously fluffed her perfectly coiffed hair with her manicured fingers, and lowered her voice. "Your father's campaign is at a crucial point. We need everyone on their best behavior."

"Is that so?" I crossed my arms. "Is he still planning to marry me off to help his campaign? I hope the suitor's family sent enough goats. I'm worth at least double what you got for Quinn."

"*Reagan.*" My father's stern voice vibrated through the hallway.

It was a fucking McKinley Family Reunion out here now.

"When Daddy becomes governor," Quinn said, "it'll only be a couple of years before we'll all be off to Washington."

Pierce winked. "Reagan, Quincy, and Pierce—back in the White House. The press will have a field day with that."

My father placed a strong hand on Pierce's shoulder. "First let me claim my seat as governor.

We will talk more about the big picture when the time comes." He turned to me with a calculated smile. "I am so glad to see that you have come to your senses and decided to join us, Reagan."

These people—my *family*—were like strangers to me. My heart ached for Dare and his family. Dalia, Dax, and Dash had felt like my real siblings from the moment I'd met them. I couldn't stand the thought of losing them...of losing Dare.

Everything that was going on with him was fully my father's fault.

"I'm not joining you," I said. "I'm only here because you need to undo what you did."

He smoothed out his tuxedo jacket and cocked his head. "Once again, I haven't the slightest idea what you are referring to, Reagan."

"You know exactly what I'm talking about," I said, raising my voice. "Everything that has happened to Dare in the last month is because of you, and you are going to put a stop to it now. TONIGHT."

My mother glanced behind her at the reporter lurking in the doorway and shot him her best fake smile. "Now is hardly the time to be shouting accusations at your father," she said through clenched teeth. "Come inside and have a drink, Reagan."

I returned her saccharine smile. "I don't drink anymore, Mother. Are you going to offer me some pills for my hysteria next? Let me save you the trouble—I'm clean. I don't solve problems with alcohol and pills anymore, numbing myself like everyone else in this family." At those words, Quinn and my mother both reached for their matching set of pearls. I couldn't help but let out a bitter laugh.

My mother's eyes widened in shock, but she mirrored my laughter. Her lips quirked up in discomfort as the phony high-pitched sound rang through the hallway. The nosy reporter smiled, looking completely fooled. We looked like one big, happy family.

What a crock.

"Whatever it is that you wish to say to your father, I have the right to hear as well." My mother's fingers were working tirelessly now, smoothing her hair over and over again.

"Why?" I scoffed. "The only decisions you ever make for this family are what shade of white to paint the walls and which designer to wear." From successful lawyer to my father's number one yes-woman—it was so freaking sad how far she'd fallen.

"Reagan." My father motioned toward the back of the house. "Why don't we step into my office and speak privately." Then he turned to my sister. "Have Rosa fix your mother a drink."

I followed him, passing the heavy oak door that

my mother had imported from Bali last year. Wood found on this continent apparently didn't cut it when it came to the mayor's home office.

My father didn't bother sitting. The moment he closed the door, he turned on me. "I will not have you provoking your mother, crashing this event, and spouting your outlandish accusations."

I clenched my jaw, matching his cold stare with my own. "There is nothing outlandish about them. You had Daren Wilde released from prison. That's a fact. And you need to put him back where you found him." I raised my chin. "You cannot control who I love, nor what I do anymore. And you've hurt people with this stupid, dangerous stunt. You need to fix it."

He sighed dramatically and I swore he almost rolled his eyes. "I do not understand why you seem so intent on ruining our family with this fling of yours," he said. "You have had your fun, proved your point. It is time to be done with your little rebellion." He pointed a finger at me. "Harvard. You say the word, get yourself back on track, and I will make it all go away."

"I'm not proving a fucking point. I LOVE Dare." My hands were fisted at my sides, my teeth gritted. Why didn't he get it? What Dare and I had wasn't some fling. It was complicated, crazy, wild-at-heart love. "This isn't about you. This isn't me rebelling. This is me having a life of my own.

Something that you are just going to have to accept."

Crossing his arms, he shrugged. "Well then, I guess there is nothing I can do for you."

Fuck.

"I can go to the press." I didn't want to, honestly, but I'd do it if I had to. I had nothing else to bargain with because I wasn't willing to give up Dare. Or my freedom.

His eyes narrowed. "Make sure you are prepared for the consequences of your actions if you make such an unwise choice."

Our eyes were locked, and I just shook my head, done with him. Turning, I opened the door, but when I saw who was standing in the hall, my blood froze.

No. Fucking. Way.

I slammed the door, my breathing reduced to quick, ragged puffs that matched my racing pulse. "What the hell is HE doing here?"

My father frowned. "Who?"

"You know exactly who I'm talking about!" I clenched my hands to keep them from shaking. "*Why is he here?*"

He sighed and rubbed his temple. "*Reagan…*"

"I'm sorry, is my question too bothersome for you?" I seethed. "Because seeing the guy who raped me walk around my parents' home like he owns the damn place is pretty fucking *bothersome* to me!"

"The Fitzgerald family is one of the most prestigious in the state, Reagan. As a former governor, Senator Fitzgerald's endorsement means more than you can imagine for my campaign."

"More than your daughter's well-being?" My eyes stung, but I took a few deep breaths and forced back the tears. The last thing I wanted to do right now was shed anymore tears over Jackson. He'd already gotten far more than he deserved.

"Friends in high places make a campaign successful. The senator will practically guarantee my win." My father's eyes darkened as he nodded at me. "And his son is part of the package. Jack is helping out on my campaign as he builds toward his own future in politics. You will have to make nice."

My knees buckled and the room began to sway. "Make...*nice?*" I choked out the words. "I can't believe you're...oh, my god. He didn't push me off the swing at the playground! *He raped me.*"

"Malicious intent on his part has never been proven," he said coolly.

"BECAUSE YOU HELPED COVER IT UP!" Seeing red, breathing fire, I tried to reign myself in. "Forget it. I don't need this. I'm no longer part of the McKinley Family Theatre. This puppet has cut her fucking strings."

"*Reagan.*" There was a sharp warning in his voice. "Do not make the mistake of walking out on this family again. You will regret it."

"See, that's the thing, *Dad*," I said. "I won't. I'm done here." I headed for the door, Jackson be damned. Fuck him if he was still out there. Fuck them all.

My father had never bothered being a father in any real way. He just played the part in pictures and at press conferences. Politics had always come first in his heart, and I was only ever valuable as a prop to help further his career. I shuddered, realizing that he would even hand me over to Jackson if it meant pleasing the senator.

"I am warning you, Reagan Allison McKinley."

Pausing in the doorway, I turned my head and said, "Stay the hell away from Dare."

My bravado lasted all the way to the foyer. I called the elevator, pressing the button over and over again with shaking fingers as I heard someone call my name.

No. Not someone.

Him.

I could never forget that voice or the way my name sounded on his lips.

My entire body began to tremble as I prayed for the elevator to hurry up. Finally, it opened and a laughing group of women from one of my mother's charities filed past me. I rushed in, hitting the button for the ground floor as Jackson's voice grew louder. Just before the door slid shut, he came into view.

Our eyes connected for a brief moment, causing my throat to close and my breath to catch. Then the doors slid shut, blessedly letting me breathe again, and the elevator took me away to safety.

nine
Dare

My mom moved around the kitchen, her long dark hair pulled up and off her face. She wiped and rewiped every surface, as if they'd gotten dirty since she'd cleaned yesterday. And every day before that.

Her nervous energy was putting me on edge.

For the past three weeks—ever since I'd been released—she'd been taking care of me in my new apartment. Dash had my stuff packed up and sent from Paris, and it had arrived about a week ago. My mom had put everything away.

Everything except my art stuff. That was mine to do, and I wasn't ready yet.

My right hand throbbed in the splint, and I angrily shoved away all thoughts about art. Especially mine. Only time would tell whether that hand would ever be of any use again.

Fucking time.

Time was screwing with my life. Time was

keeping me from Ree. Time was the only thing my dad had before I caught up with him.

"Mom," I said quietly, my voice making her jump.

Pressing a shaky hand to her chest, she turned toward me. "Dear god, Dare. Wear a bell, would you?" She wiped the hair off her forehead with the back of her hand. "What are you doing up? You feeling okay?"

"I'm fine," I said. A lie. I was pissed as hell about everything, but I shoved it down as deep as I could. "We're not done talking."

"I am." She turned her back on me and went over to scrub the sink. Again. "That conversation is over."

"Toronto."

"No." She smashed the sponge down onto the counter and whipped around, her eyes flashing. "I am not leaving you here to deal with all this by yours—"

"Have you talked to him?"

Her eyes widened, and she pressed her lips together.

I shook my head. "This is why you have to go. He'll suck you in again. And I can't keep you safe...from yourself."

Her shoulders sagged and she leaned against the counter. "I just...I don't know what it is about him. I'm sorry, Dare. I can't help it."

"I know. Which is why you have to go. Dalia and Dax are safe out west and, lucky for us, he seems to only have it out for me."

"Not lucky for you." There was real fear in her eyes.

I laughed, a hollow, cold sound. "I can handle him. If he's only focused on me, then I don't have to worry about any of you. But he'll try to hurt me by hurting you, Mom. You know he will. I bought you a ticket on the train leaving tomorrow morning. Julie will meet you at the station in Toronto." I walked slowly across the kitchen and put my arm around her shaking shoulders. "I'll be okay. I promise."

"I'm sorry." Her voice was muffled, small. "This is all my fault."

"No," I said, squeezing her tight. "It's him. It's always been him." I looked around the pristine kitchen. "You should pack. The train leaves early."

There wasn't anything she could say to make me change my mind, and she knew that, so she gave me one last squeeze and then left the room without another word. We'd been arguing about this all day. She was the last loose end that needed tying up before I could take care of him. Once and for all. I'd let her stay this long in part because I knew she felt responsible for what had happened to me, and also because I'd needed the help.

As much as I hated to admit it.

But my strength was returning and the longer she stayed, the more likely it was my father would show up, probably sooner than I would be ready.

And, this time, I had to be ready.

Because no one I loved was safe while he was alive and free. Not my mom. Not the Terrors. Not Rex. And especially not Ree.

Ree.

It was killing me to not have her here with me, but I couldn't risk it. I couldn't risk her.

The fingers of my good hand skimmed the outline of the phone in my pocket. Rex had been checking in with me daily, not only to see how I was doing, but to let me know how Ree was. I'd lost count of how many times an hour I reached for my cell, itching to dial his number. Just on the off chance I'd hear her voice in the background. I hadn't yet, knowing full well that I wouldn't be able to stay away if I did.

Cursing under my breath, I slammed my hand on the counter. Fuck, I needed a distraction. Something to do. Anything to get my mind off Ree.

But my mom had done everything.

Everything but my studio.

All of my art supplies and paintings were still boxed up, collecting dust. It was the last room that needed unpacking, and I'd been putting it off even though I needed to go through my paintings for a show Rex was setting up for me. Some gallery manager was coming by in a couple of days. Though I desperately needed the money, I hadn't even wanted to get started on that. It was just one more reminder of what I couldn't do right now, and might not be able to ever do again. Why torture myself with one more thing I couldn't have?

But, fuck it all, I was desperate for a distraction. And desperate times...

I walked down the hall, and stood in the doorway, staring at the piled up boxes. So much potential in this room. Too much. And as much as it pained me to even think about my art right now, if anything was going to keep my mind off Ree it was this.

Art had once been the sole love of my life. Until I met Ree.

But the two were so entwined now—my love for art and my love for her. They crissed and crossed, wrapped around my heart and mind. Ree was art. Art was Ree. They'd become one and the same, and damn it all, unpacking these boxes was doing nothing BUT making me think about her.

"FUCK!" I yelled into the empty room.

The sound bounced off the colorless walls, ricocheting like gunfire. I yanked out blank

canvases and launched them across the room.
Grabbing tubes of paint, I hurled them as hard as
I could, one after the other until the box was
empty.

The cap had flown off of a tube of cadmium
red, splattering the white walls and scattered
canvases with splotches of red.

And I froze.

Horrifying images from thirteen years ago
flashed through my mind. I'd found out that one
of my dad's men was an undercover cop and had
accidentally let it slip. Dad dragged me to a
meeting, jumped the guy, and put the gun in my
hand.

"You get to do the honors, kid," he'd said.
"Since you discovered it." Then he leaned in close
to me, his eyes gleaming as he looked at the
doomed man, beaten beyond recognition already.
"It's like winning the fucking lottery, isn't it,
Junior?"

My hands shook like mad, and there was no way
I was going to pull the trigger, even though
everyone was staring at me, goading me on. A
fucking twelve-year-old kid.

I lowered my gun, breathing hard, no idea what
was in store for me. My dad would not take this
lightly—my refusal—but I just couldn't do it.

My father turned his gun on me. "Fucking
shoot the narc or I'll fucking shoot you."

I closed my eyes and waited, the gun growing heavier by the second. Water dripped from across the room, and the only other sound I heard was footsteps getting closer.

The first hit knocked me clean off my feet, and the gun skittered out of my hands. My forehead stung like crazy, warmth washing over it, and I was reaching up to clutch my head when something hard hit my arm. I heard the bone crack a moment before the pain registered, and I started screaming.

He leaned over and smacked my face. "Shut up, little girl. Such a fucking pussy." He hauled me to my feet as I clutched my arm to my body, then he put his foot on my ass and pushed. I went flying forward, arms outstretched to catch myself. My body crumpled to the ground, the bones of my arm ripping through skin as I howled in pain.

"Leave the kid alone, you fucking psycho!" The words were spat out, drops of blood splattering as if to punctuate.

I lay there panting on the ground, blackness crowding the edges of my vision, as my father looked over his shoulder at the cop.

"How fucking noble of you, Officer Douglas, trying to save my worthless son." My dad stalked toward him slowly, menacingly, his finger caressing the trigger of his gun as he raised it and aimed.

Waves of pain crashed over me, each one bigger than the last, and nausea rose higher and higher. Darkness shrouded me, my eyes closed, and everything sounded far, far away.

"Too bad there's no one here to save you, you son of a bitch." My dad's voice came at me from the end of a long tunnel. The shot that rang out was the last thing I heard that night.

I heard the echo of that gunshot in my nightmares for years.

Everyone involved had been silenced in one way or another. My dad had gotten away with it, and the murder had gone unsolved.

But not anymore.

THIS could bring him down.

I could go to the police, tell them what I knew, what I'd seen.

The only problem? I had no proof and wasn't witness to the crime—I hadn't actually seen him shoot the cop.

My vision blurred as I stared at the mess I'd made. And then it hit me.

I had no proof...*but Stanzi did*. If he was still alive. And if I could find the little parasite.

Taking a deep breath, I stepped back a few feet, almost staggering under the immensity of what I was thinking about doing. If I turned in my dad, I'd also be implicating myself. Taking away my father's freedom could cost me my own.

Was it a price I was willing to pay to keep my family and Ree safe?

Hell yes.

THIS was what I'd had over him.

It hadn't been an ace I was holding the first time I went to see him. It had been a goddamn wild card.

Deadly calm spread throughout my body, and I felt more certain of this than I had of most decisions I'd ever made in my life.

My father was going down by MY hand. Finally.

I'd spent a lifetime being his prey, but I was about to become his predator.

And the best part?

He was never going to see it coming.

ten
Reagan

"I still can't believe you get to live with Rex Vogel." Arianna Saxon straightened an abstract painting of bright blues, oranges, and reds, then stepped back to look at it again. She tucked a strand of long, dark auburn hair behind her ear. "I mean, he's a freaking legend. You've got to be the luckiest person I know."

"I'm not living *with* him," I said, trying really hard not to roll my eyes. When I'd called Sabine to ask if she'd let the gallery host Dare's show, she'd immediately said yes and offered me another job. That woman was definitely up for sainthood, and I was pretty sure I'd need to name my first child after her for all the things she'd done for me. "He has a separate apartment over his studio which I'm renting."

A new show was opening at La Période Bleue in a few days, and we were putting the finishing touches on it. Then Dare's exhibition would follow. Sabine was in Paris, overseeing the big showcase she'd originally hired me to run, and then she was spending the next six months scouting talent in Europe. In her absence, she'd left Arianna to manage the New York gallery.

I'd have been lying if I said that hadn't stung.

But I couldn't blame her. Arianna had been working at the gallery for over a year. Not to mention, Sabine had made these plans to spend time in Europe long before I'd bailed on her in Paris again. She'd simply moved up her departure date so she could take over for me first.

And Arianna was good. At twenty-six she'd built up an impressive list of clientele, and was already looking for a space in the city to open her own gallery in the next year or so. She had an incredible eye for talent—so much so that I had no doubt the paintings we were hanging would sell on opening night.

She was everything I wanted to be.

"But then again, maybe *I'm* the luckiest person because you introduced me to Rex and he's been telling me about the artist we're showing next. He's taking me there tomorrow to see the paintings and meet the guy." She brushed some imaginary dust off another painting's frame. "I have such a good feeling about this guy and I haven't even seen his work yet. But if Sabine and Rex like it, it's got to be something special, don't you think?"

"Without a doubt." I liked Arianna, but the girl had talked about nothing but Rex since he'd picked me up after my first day of work. He'd come to make the connection with Arianna, so it would look like he'd been the one to arrange the show instead of me.

And it was fine. I was dealing.

Besides, Rex had been incredibly kind since he'd taken me under his wing. He stayed up late with me when I didn't want to sleep because my nightmares had returned. He accompanied me to AA meetings and helped recommend a good therapist. But more than anything, he was a shoulder to lean on and an empathetic ear when I needed to talk.

If Sabine was my fairy godmother, Rex was my fairy godfather.

Most importantly, he kept me connected to Dare. Not that Rex ever said much about him, but I knew he was keeping tabs on Dare, and if anything happened to him, I would know.

It wasn't much, but it was *something*.

At this point, I had to take anything I could get.

Dare and his family had completely cut me off—no one was answering my calls or texts. I couldn't get anything out of them. And Rex just looked at me like his heart was broken every time I asked. So I stopped asking.

Arianna pivoted in the middle of the gallery,

taking in each painting as she scoped out the room.

"Perfect," she finally said, and I breathed a sigh of relief. I was ready to go home.

Even though I wasn't spending every moment at his bedside anymore, I was still eating, sleeping, and breathing Dare. He was a part of every aspect of my life.

I couldn't get away from thoughts about him anywhere I went—not at the gallery, not at Rex's.

And, truth be told, I didn't really want to anyway.

"Rex?" The screen door banged closed behind me as I strode into his silent studio. I was a little late tonight, but it was odd that he wasn't inside. Although the cast hadn't come off his arm yet, he still spent all day painting after I helped set up the canvases and paints each morning. Every night when I got home from the gallery, he was always here, hard at work.

It was so strange to think of this place as home, but it felt more like home to me than any other place, save for Dare's. And Rex had welcomed me as if I were his own daughter.

Setting my bag down on the stairs, I walked through the studio and deeper into the house. Rex was in the kitchen trying to wrestle a pot of water from the sink to the stove.

With one arm.

Hurrying over, I took the pot and placed it on the stove.

"Look, I know my cooking skills are lacking," I said, "but are they so bad you've been forced to fend for yourself with only one good arm?"

He laughed—a wonderful, rich sound that rolled around the room and wrapped me in warmth—and shook his head. "I thought I'd give you a break tonight. Make dinner for once. I miss it."

I glanced at his sling. "You'll be back at it again soon. In the meantime, you're teaching me how to cook. That's a worthwhile endeavor, isn't it? Even if I screw up every dish?"

"Not *every* dish." He laughed again when I raised an eyebrow at him. "You're getting better every time."

"So, tell me, what are we making tonight?" Walking over to the sink to wash my hands, I spotted the cheese, milk, and butter on the counter.

Oh, shit. I knew what this meant even before he spoke.

"My famous macaroni and cheese." Rex opened a cupboard and pulled out a grater. "You haven't lived until you've had this dish. It's my secret recipe that only a few other people know."

The water ran cold over my hands. My stomach tightened, and I was sure I would not be able to eat. But I didn't want Rex to feel bad—he obviously didn't know. He'd been so careful to not mention Dare—if he'd had any inkling of the significance of this dish, I knew he'd never have planned to make it.

I couldn't do anything but force a smile and try to get through this without bawling my eyes out.

Why did everything have to be so fucking hard?

I turned on the burner under the pot of water and started grating the cheese, every slide down the grater feeling like it was taking off a layer of my skin. Damn it. I needed to focus on something else or I was going to salt the water with my tears.

"How's the painting going?"

Struggling a little to keep the box steady, Rex opened the pasta. "It's going," he said with a sigh. "It's a process. It always is, but even more so with one arm."

"At least it's your left." As soon as the words came out of my mouth, I cursed myself. Because we were both now thinking about Dare and his damaged right hand. Shit. "I meant—"

"I know what you meant." Rex's voice was gentle. "It's okay, Ree." He paused and I glanced over at him. "You wanna know?"

I nodded, my eyes wide. Yes, fuck it all, I

wanted to know. No matter how much it hurt.

"He's...okay. He's been going to physical therapy, doing exercises, and still wearing a splint. He's getting his range of motion back bit by bit. He's planning to get back to the canvas this week."

I'd been holding my breath the whole time he'd been talking, and now that he was done I released it, pressing my tongue hard against my teeth as I forced the tears back down. I was so freaking relieved that he was getting back to painting—I hadn't even realized how stressed I'd been about it.

"I'm...that's really great to hear," I said, then turned back to the stove, and poured the pasta into the boiling water.

Rex touched my shoulder. "I'll be back in a minute. There's something I want to show you."

Melting the butter and mixing in the flour, I tried to focus on the sauce and not Dare. Which was virtually impossible because all I could think about was the first time I'd made this sauce with him and the things he'd said and done to me.

My heart felt like it was breaking all over again.

The door to Rex's studio opened.

Without even turning around, I said, "You know, if there's something you want me to see in your studio, I can come out there as soon as I put this in the oven."

He didn't respond.

"Rex?" I glanced over my shoulder.

But Rex wasn't standing there.

Dare was.

eleven
Reagan

My knees went weak at the sight of him, my vision blurred. The wooden spoon dropped out of my hand, spattering sauce all over the floor.

"What...?" I swallowed hard, hands shaking, chest aching, my whole body feeling pulled toward Dare with a force greater than gravity.

But I stayed rooted in place, not sure of what his appearance meant.

He was looking at me like he was just as tortured by my nearness as I was by his. Frozen, we stared at each other, but then he came forward, opening a drawer to pull out another spoon, and then reaching around me toward the stove.

"You're burning the sauce." His lips were right next to my ear, his arms practically wrapped around me so he could reach the pan. Unable to keep from touching him, I leaned into him, feeling the hard length of his body pressing into mine.

His muscles stiffened, and he shuddered against me.

Turning my head to look up into his stormy eyes, I breathed him in, wishing I could drown in his scent as I tried to make sense of what the hell was going on. Why had he shown up all of a sudden? Was he finally willing to accept help?

Please, please let him have come to his senses.

"Why are you…I don't…" God, I sounded like an idiot. Just say it, already. "What are you doing here?"

He leaned down, his breath brushing my cheek, spreading warmth across it like color on canvas. "I can't stay away, Ree."

His words left me breathless. "Then don't," I said in a throaty voice I barely recognized.

I moved without thinking, pulling him toward me, crashing his lips to mine. He claimed me, his mouth hard and wanting, his tongue meeting mine, licking and tasting as if he were discovering me for the very first time.

I heard the spoon clattering on the stovetop, and then he was pinning me tightly against the wall of muscle that was his body. He left my mouth and kissed his way down my neck, hungrily moaning my name over and over again, making my skin tingle. I let my head fall back, for a brief instant allowing Dare to take over all my thoughts, completely losing myself in him.

I'd missed him so fucking much, craved the feel of his lips, ached to have his arms wrapped around me, dreamed of hearing his voice. His presence had the power to leave me senseless, his kisses blew my mind. I wanted to just give in to him, to surrender to the sensations I'd been missing since we'd said goodbye in Amsterdam.

But something nagged at the back of my mind, refusing to let go.

Placing my hands on his chest, I pushed away from him, my whole body screaming at me for stopping the kaleidoscope of sensations spurred on by his touch.

This was more important.

"What is this?" I waved my hand back and forth between us. "Are you back? Is that why you're here?"

His face hardened and he opened his mouth as if to say something, but then shook his head. "It doesn't matter," he said as he slipped his fingers into my waistband and pulled me hard against him. "I miss you."

"It DOES matter." I thrust away from him, feeling anger stir deep within my chest. "Are you going to let me help?"

Gaze like granite, he shook his head once.

Over Dare's shoulder I saw Rex round the corner. He halted when he saw us, his eyes growing wide.

I glared up at Dare. "*Fine*. You know where the door is."

I shoved him away from me as hard as I could and ran out of the kitchen, into the studio, taking the stairs two at a time, tripping over my bag and banging my shin against the steps in the process. Cursing all the way up to my apartment, I swung the door shut behind me with as much force as I could.

When I didn't hear it slam, I turned to find Dare in its way.

"Get. Out." I spat each word at him.

In a few quick strides, he was across the room, reaching for me. "Ree—"

"No, Dare. Stop fucking with me." I took a step back, trying to untangle from his grasp. "I can't take it. Go away and don't come back until you've got your head on straight."

His eyes flashed as he gripped my shoulder with his one good hand. "You don't understand," he said, his words laced with anguish. "As long as he's out there and we're together, your life is in danger." Pain slashed across his face. "I can't risk you, Ree. He's out to take everything from me. But if he doesn't know about you, then he can't get to you."

"He can't take me away from you." I reached out to touch his face. "I'm yours. Only yours.

Always yours, Dare."

With our lips mere inches apart, I could hear his breath hitch then felt him inhale sharply. His eyes scorched mine, a thousand different expressions flashing through them in a single instant. When his gaze descended to my mouth, heat flooded through my core, his ravenous look dizzying me.

Our mouths collided, my body coming alive as his tongue tangled with mine. His hand fisted in my hair, holding me in place, a willing captive. Tingling spread from between my thighs, up my abdomen, creating a ripple effect through the rest of my body, drowning my soul in so much light and warmth. Relishing in the feel of him against me, I felt as if I were waking up from a long, dark dream.

He ran his fingers through my hair, gripped my head, and broke our kiss. His wild eyes met mine. "You are mine, Ree," he said. "Don't you ever forget that." A deep growl rose within his chest as his lips found mine again, making me ache in all the right places, sending my hands to the hem of his shirt to lift it over his head.

When he pulled back to let me tug it off his head, I gasped at what I saw. Healing cuts marred the perfect landscape of his torso. As he carefully slid the tee over his splint and tossed it to the floor, I gently ran my fingers along his side.

"Oh my god, Dare." My words were just a

horrified whisper. "What did he do to you?"

"Nothing he hasn't done before." Then he held up his splinted hand, wincing slightly. "Well, except for this. This was a special treat just for me. To take away my art."

Tears slipped down my cheeks, and I didn't even bother trying to stop them this time. My heart wrenched at the sight and I hated that I didn't know what to say to make it all better. What could you say to someone whose father was bound and determined to destroy his life?

So I just took his good hand in mine, led him to the couch, and sat him down. Then I went into the kitchen and filled a small towel with ice. I searched for a rubber band to keep it closed, but couldn't find one. We would have to do without.

I knew it was completely futile to put ice on his hand at this point, but I had to do *something*. And I needed a moment to gather myself. Seeing his beautiful body so bruised and beaten…it killed me.

A couple of deep breaths later, I walked back out to the couch, my makeshift icepack in hand. Dare's dark eyes followed me across the room, until I was standing between his knees.

"Are your legs okay?" I asked.

He started to nod, and when I slid onto his lap, my skirt riding up as I straddled his legs, a slow, sly grin grew across his face. I gently lifted his hurt hand, placed it in my lap, and lowered the ice onto it. His eyes never left my face, and an incredibly tender expression filled them, growing warmer with each passing second.

"Ree," he said, caressing my name, making my heart swell.

God, I loved him.

I leaned forward to kiss his delicious lips, but before mine could touch his, the towel slipped out of my hand, spilling ice across our laps. I gasped at the sudden cold contact on my bare legs, and quickly began scooping up the cubes and placing them back on the towel.

Dare laughed, then immediately pressed his hand to his ribs.

"Fuck, that kills," he said. "Please don't do anything adorable to make me laugh."

"No laughing and no adorableness. Got it." He hadn't said a single thing about first-aid, though. "Where does it hurt?" Armed with a cube in each hand, I reached out and skated the ice along his skin, slowly trailing it over to his ribs. "Here?"

Dare sucked in a sharp breath, his tongue snaking out to lick his lips as he watched me work. "That's right," he said. "But, all of a sudden, it's beginning to feel better. Go figure."

"And how about here?" I moved toward his chest and glided the melting cubes down his stomach. Water dripped over the ridges of his abs as his muscles tensed beneath my touch. I slid my tongue up the center of his body, and licked every drop, savoring his smooth skin and kissing every cut. Then I followed the warm path with ice.

When the cubes skimmed his nipples, he groaned, his gaze darkening with desire. "God, I love it when you play doctor."

"You think they teach this at med school?" I grazed his right nipple with my teeth and looked up at him, grinning wickedly as the ache between my thighs began to throb again.

The growing bulge in his pants inspired me to head south. I teased the sharp triangle of muscle peeking out from the waistband of his jeans, dipping lower and lower over his hot skin until he moaned and let his head fall back against the couch.

"If I could rip off your clothes right now, I would," he said. "But, today, you're going to have to do it for me." He shifted the ice-filled towel to the cushion beside him. "Stand up."

I pressed my throbbing core against his hardness before sliding backward off his legs. He let out a ravenous groan at the contact, his good hand clenched at his side.

"Unbutton your shirt." His gaze burned through me, making me feel exposed before I even started the show.

One by one, I released each shiny button, my

eyes never leaving Dare's, until my turquoise blouse hung open.

"Take it off," he said, and I shrugged the shirt off my shoulders. "Now your bra."

I reached behind me and undid the clasp, my nipples hardening in anticipation of what was to come. The fabric went limp around me, but my crossed arms kept it in place.

Dare shifted in his seat. I didn't think his eyes could get any darker, but they now flashed a deep onyx—the color of sin. "Let it fall. I want to see all of you."

As I moved my hands to my sides, the black silk tumbled away, leaving me bare from the waist up. And so fucking turned on all I wanted to do was rip off the rest of my clothes and jump him.

Without waiting for his instructions, I dipped my hands into the waistband of my skirt, gliding it over my hips and down my legs until it was a puddle of fabric on the floor.

"Someone's being naughty." Dare shook his head and smirked. "And eager."

Understatement of the millennium.

I wanted him...*yesterday*. And the day before. And every single moment of my life.

I yearned to make up for every second we'd been apart.

He licked his bottom lip and raked his gaze down my body, leaving a trail of heat over my skin. "Come here," he said, his voice hoarse with want, his pants now straining.

I stepped in between his knees and he slid his good hand up my stomach to cup my right breast, his thumb teasing my nipple into a tight peak. "So beautiful." He murmured the words like he was talking more to himself than to me, gently flicking the bud before moving down my side, over my ass, to my inner thigh. He ran his hand up the sensitive flesh so slowly I was moaning even before he reached between my legs and brushed his fingers over my panties.

"Soaked through. Just like I thought." He slipped his index finger under the silky material and dipped into my heat, releasing a thunderous groan. "Fuck, Ree. You're so ready for me."

I nodded, and Dare pulled his hand away, replacing it with my own. "Feel how incredibly sexy you are." He guided my fingers over my wet, velvety folds, before withdrawing them and sucking one into his mouth. Shutting his eyes, he flicked his tongue over me, moaning as he savored me on his tongue.

"Remove your panties," he said, hooking two fingers through the thin strap that wrapped around my hips. "*Slowly.*"

I did as he asked, my eyes never leaving his even when I bent over to pick them up. I held them out to him.

"Fuck," he groaned the word, swallowing hard and fisting the fabric in his hand as he took me in. "Get over here." He patted his lap. "Now."

I slid back onto his lap, straddling him again, my throbbing core completely bared to him. The tingling that had bloomed in that sweet spot had spread throughout my whole body, all the way to my fingers and toes.

Dare picked up an ice cube and traced my phoenix with it, raising goosebumps on my skin as lines of water rolled over my hip. He followed the drips down my leg with the ice, then brought it to the inside of my thigh and trailed it upward.

The sensation, combined with the anticipation of where he was headed, had me gasping and writhing as he inched it closer and closer to my center. The moment the cold touched my clit, the tingling intensified, sending jolts of electricity throughout my body. An instant later, warmth enveloped my ache when he began to massage me with his thumb.

Spreading his knees and opening me even wider, he did it again. Cold, warmth. Cold, warmth. My hips started rocking to his rhythm as I panted his name, quickly edging toward an explosion of ecstasy.

"I need to taste you. Up on your feet." He grunted out the order, and I rose, my feet digging into the couch cushions, my pulsing clit level with his mouth. "Closer."

I braced my hands on the wall and tipped my hips toward him so my ache was millimeters away, which brought the throbbing between my legs to an all-time high. His eyes locked on mine, he put the cube in his mouth, then wrapped his lips around my clit. I gasped at the juxtaposition of the cold ice and his hot mouth, and moaned at the contrast between the softness of his lips and the pressure of his tongue.

"So goddamn delicious, Ree."

When his teeth grazed me, I knew I was past the point of no return. He sucked and nipped, winding me up tightly. The hot, cold, hot, cold, had me spiraling up and up until my feet left the ground and I touched stars. Or, at least, saw them blinding and bright behind my eyes.

When he slid his hand up my thigh and slipped two fingers inside me, I fisted his hair and begged for more and more—faster, harder, deeper...*please*. I was overwhelmed with Dare, my mind and body dominated by him—inside and out. As he brought my body up to the highest heights and then sent me flying over the edge, I cried out his name over and over again, love and lust lacing my words.

When the tremors had passed and the quaking of my legs had subsided, I lowered myself back down and kissed him with everything I was. Everything *he* was to me.

Then I grabbed the waistband of his jeans and unzipped them, my hands immediately hitting hot skin.

"I'll never tire of your commando style," I said, shifting the denim down farther to free him completely. "Who needs Calvin Klein when you've got Dare Wilde?"

He laughed, then immediately grimaced. "You can't make me laugh. I already told you that."

"Shit." I placed a gentle hand on his bruised side. "Maybe it's good I'm not an actual doctor."

"I don't know," he said, a wicked grin stretching across his face, "your treatments are the best I've ever had. I'll gladly take anything you prescribe."

"In that case..." Dare moaned as I took him into my hands and stroked his rock-hard length.

"Oh god, Ree." His sweet and dirty moans made my ache come alive again. "I need to be inside you," he said, his voice sinfully low and husky. "I want to bury myself all the way and make you come apart for me again."

God, those words.

I straddled his legs, and kissed him hungrily as I lowered myself onto him. He moaned, sucking my bottom lip into his mouth, then biting down on the tender flesh as I began to rock my hips. The feeling of him deep inside me sent my head spinning again.

Dare gripped my hip with one hand, guiding my

pace, digging his fingers in as he moaned at our connection. "Christ, Ree. You're so tight, so wet."

Speeding up his rhythm, he pounded into me, over and over, each time sinking farther, thrusting harder, kissing wilder. I arched my back and ground my hips faster, matching his tempo. Panting, moaning, gasping.

"There's nothing hotter than hearing those sweet sounds while I watch you ride me," Dare said. His eyes never left mine, imprisoning me, keeping me locked under his spell. "Except maybe listening to you moan my name as you come. I want to hear you let go." The words were equally an appeal and a demand. "Come for me— *with* me."

The friction as I slid over him, up and down, back and forth, had me riding another wave up with him. Up and up and up, until we were both breaking apart and exploding together.

Our bodies collided; our hearts crashed into each other.

Two parts. One whole.

Dare collapsed against the back of the couch, panting hard, and I folded over him, my head against his shoulder as I tried to catch my sprinting pulse. Our hearts spoke the same language, and our bodies glistened with a light coat of post-bliss sweat.

Needing to touch as much of him as I could, I

wanted nothing more than to stay cuddled up against him. However, considering I'd probably aggravated his injuries, I slid off his lap and onto the cushions next to him and settled for lacing our fingers together as I draped my legs over his.

When we'd caught our breath, I said, "So, what are we going to do about your father?"

His jaw tightened and his lips thinned, but he didn't speak.

I turned to look at him. "Dare?"

"I have something on him." He stared across the room, not meeting my gaze.

"What?"

"He killed a cop," he said, still refusing to look at me. "Thirteen years ago. And he got away with it. Until now, that is."

"Oh, my god. You mean the Douglas case?" I slipped my legs off of his and sat up. "That was *your father?*"

It had been all over the news when it happened. Danny Douglas had been an undercover cop working on a drug case for over a year, trying to bust a big drug runner. My father had just begun getting into politics at the time, so it was all he could talk about with anybody. It had been a huge blow to have the case go unsolved.

"Holy shit, Dare," I said.

"I know."

"So why not take it to the police?"

"I didn't actually see him do it, and I don't have any tangible proof. If I'm going to make him go away, I need proof. I'm working on that now. My dad's well aware that I know about it because I was there."

"You—OH SHIT." My eyes widened as I realized the implications of all this. "If you were there and you've known about it all this time, you might be charged as an accessory." God, did the bounds of what his father had done to him have no limits?

Dare nodded, still not looking at me. "Yeah." He took a deep breath, ran his hand through his hair. "But it'll put the bastard behind bars for life."

"Then you can't do it." I stood up, grabbed my clothes and started yanking them on. "There has to be something else. You can leave an anonymous tip. Mail the proof to the police. That way you can't be implicated."

Dare let out a bitter laugh. "Are you kidding? I'll be the first person my dad points his finger at. That bastard is not going to go down without a fight."

"Yes, but—"

"I have to do this, Ree. It's the only way to keep everyone safe." His eyes finally met mine. "I need to keep you safe," he said. "But first I have to actually find the guy who has the proof."

"Who is it? And what does he have?"

"His name is Mike Stanzione, but everyone calls him Stanzi." Dare's face contorted in disgust. "And he has photographs. My father has always been inclined to keep mementos of what he considers to be his greatest accomplishments. Stanzi was his record keeper."

I shuddered at the thought. The whole situation—this plan of Dare's and the crime he hoped to unearth—screamed BAD IDEA to me. Too many things could go wrong. The stakes were too high, the risk too terrible.

"There must be some other way, Dare. NOT this. Just like you can't lose me, I can't lose you." I placed my hand on his arm and squeezed my fingers around him. "Do you understand that? This isn't just about *you*. It's about *us*. You could go to prison!"

"I have no choice, Ree. If there was some other option, I'd take it. But this is guaranteed to work."

"*Let me help.*" My words were coming louder and faster as my panic level skyrocketed. "You don't have to fucking do this on your own. Between the two of us, we can come up something. Maybe my father—"

"*Your father* let him out. He's not going to do shit." He stood up and zipped his jeans, his eyes angry, his jaw tight. "You and I both know that." He shook his head. "I get that you don't like this,

Ree. I don't either, but it's all I've got. It's the only way I can keep him from destroying everything I love. No one is safe. Not Dalia and Dax. Not my mom. Not Dash. Not you. Look at what he did to Rex."

My eyes widened. "And what he did to you. It's not safe for you either. Who's going to protect you?" I sank down on the couch.

"That's not the way it works for me." Dare shrugged, resigned. "You can see why I have to do this, then." He picked up his shirt and pulled it over his head, cursing when the material caught on his splint.

"No," I said, "I DON'T see why you have to do it this way. That's even more reason to work together. Two minds are better than one. Three are better than two. Let's go downstairs and talk to Rex, figure something out that will not end with you going to prison."

His face was hard as he shook his head. "You don't get it, Ree."

"You're right, I don't. You can't lose me, but you won't let me help so I don't lose you. What kind of fucked-up double-standard bullshit is that?" I picked up the towel of melting ice, and stalked toward the kitchen, but then swung around to face him in the doorway. "You know what? Fine. Go on your little mission. Get the fuck out of here. If you don't value me as a full-fledged partner in your life, then I don't need this shit. Let me know when the macho bullshit has gotten you in so deep that you need my help to get out of it. Because you *will*." I turned my back on him, and stormed into the kitchen. "But until then, fuck off."

I heard the door slam a moment later, and threw the towel at the wall, scattering ice all over the kitchen.

FUCK.

Gripping the counter, I took several deep breaths, battling to regain control, my body shaking. Because the thing was, I had to find a way to save him this time. Regardless of what I'd just said. Even if he didn't want me to.

Dare had saved me in more ways than I could count.

It was my turn now.

I just had to figure out how.

twelve
Dare

"You're early," I said as I opened the door to Rex the next morning. I glanced down the street both ways. "You didn't tell her you were coming here, right?" I ushered him inside.

Rex strode in, turned around, and stared at me. Just like he had when I was fresh out of juvie and begging him to take me in again.

Shit. This was not going to go well.

"Rex—"

"Don't you *Rex* me," he said. "Are you really that stupid? Ree told me your plans." He narrowed his eyes at me. "It's a suicide mission and you know it. Look at you! Look at what that rat bastard did to you." He rattled the sling his left arm was still in. "And me! He will kill you next time, Dare. I have no doubt about that. He's leading up to it. That piece of shit has always had it out for you."

"Listen, Rex—"

"No, you listen to me. I've wanted to say this for years because it's something I don't think you know or understand." He took a deep breath and said, "He NEVER deserved you. I can't comprehend a world where someone like *him* gets to have *you* for a son." His eyes were getting redder by the minute as his gaze burned through me. "You never should've been punished with someone like that as a father. Do you know that? NEVER. You did nothing to deserve him." He shook his head, and some of his gray hair came loose from his low ponytail. He tucked a strand behind his ear and said, "I would have done anything to have a son like you. To have you for my son, Dare."

A lump rose up in my throat, and I tried hard to swallow it down.

"I can't believe you'd risk everything for that asshole. That you'd let your father take away the life you've built. The life you've earned, that you've deserved from day one."

I shook my head. "You don't understand."

"I don't understand your father? I've known him—"

"I have no choice, Rex. It's the only way to keep the family safe. To keep Ree safe. To keep *you* safe."

"You don't have to—"

"I don't?" I stalked across the room and lifted

his casted arm. "I don't have to keep you safe?"

"Dare, the whole world is not your responsibility."

"No, but my family is." I paused, that lump returning. "*You* are family. You're more of a dad than he ever was. And I will fucking do anything I can to protect you from him."

Rex pulled me into a hug, swinging his good arm around me. His familiar scent, of patchouli and paint, still smelled like comfort.

"If my dad gets even a whiff of Ree...I don't know what he'll do to her," I said. "He's hell-bent on taking away everything I love." I held up my splinted hand. "Case in point. I can't let him have her."

"But there's got to be a better way than this."

"If there was I'd be taking it in a heartbeat," I said. "But if I don't go after him, find what I need to stop him, then he'll..." I didn't want to finish that sentence. So I didn't. "How's Ree?"

Rex shrugged, his face turning to stone. "Come see for yourself."

"I can't. Last night was a stupid mistake, and she's pissed as hell at me. I have to stay away for now." I held out my hands. "Please, Rex. Just tell me how she is. I was a dick."

He considered me for a moment, then his shoulders sagged as he gave in. "She's...hurt, angry, worried, and scared." He paused. "And she loves you."

"I know."

"Dare, really think about—"

"I've thought it through. There's no other way. Trust me." A knock on the door sent my pulse up and my eyes to Rex's face. "You didn't tell her, right? Please tell me you didn't..."

"I didn't. That'll be the gallery manager I told you about." He glanced at his watch. "It's ten o'clock. She's right on time. You have the paintings ready?"

"Of course I do. What do you take me for, a total amateur?"

Rex raised an eyebrow at me. "If the beret fits..."

"Hey, I only wore it that one time." A small, bittersweet smile touched my lips. "And that was seven years ago, so it's about time you dropped it."

Rex walked over to my door, and opened it while I tried to focus. I needed this kind of distraction right now, no matter how much I didn't want it. And I really needed the income.

He ushered a tall redhead into the room, her face lighting up when her eyes landed on me. She was dressed in all black, save for a colorful scarf that wrapped around her neck, and she was looking at me like I was the artwork rather than the artist.

Great. Just what I needed.

"Dare," Rex said, sweeping his arm toward the woman, "this is Arianna Saxon."

I held out my left hand, she reached with her right, then gave an embarrassed laugh and extended her left to shake my hand.

"Sorry," she said. "I'd forgotten about your hand. How's it feeling?"

It ached like a son of a bitch.

"Fine," I said, and waved her toward my studio. "If you'd like to see the paintings, I have them all set up."

She nodded and started following my lead, with Rex trailing us.

"Oh!" she said. "I also wanted to discuss the opening. We'll start advertising it next week when our current show opens—"

"What?" I stopped and turned around to face her. "No, there can't be an opening. Or advertising." I glanced at Rex. "I thought Rex told you that."

She laughed. "Oh sure. Of course he did, but I know how nerve-wracking shows can be for some artists." She slipped her hand through my arm and started walking me toward the studio. "Don't you worry one bit. I'll be with you every step of the way, guiding you through the entire process."

"It's not that I'm nervous. We simply can't make a big deal about—"

"There's nothing for you to worry about." She gave me a gleaming smile. "I promise that you're in *very* good hands." A deep crimson blush spread over her pretty face.

Then she strode into my studio, stood stock still, and gasped.

"Oh. My. God." She did a slow circle around the room, openly gawking at my work. "This is— Rex you weren't kid—I'm...WOW." She turned to me with a big grin. "Tighten your seatbelt, Dare Wilde, because you're about to be famous. I'm going to make sure of it."

Not if I could help it.

Right now, fame was the last thing I needed.

I had to keep a low profile and not attract my father's attention in any way until I had Stanzi and was ready to strike. Then I had to find a way to not go down with him.

Fame could wait.

Everything else I was dealing with couldn't.

thirteen
Reagan

"Did you see today's Times?" Arianna had to move a mountain of contracts from the desk in front of me in order to make space for two Starbucks cups. To say that the office was an artsy warzone would be an understatement. We were being ambushed by paperwork from all sides—talent, buyers, insurance agents—the not so glamorous part of working at an art gallery.

I shook my head and waved my hand over the contract I was drawing up. "These are the only papers I've had the time to read today." Although we didn't open until noon, I'd been here since seven to prepare for the numerous shows we were hosting over the next few months. "So what kind of news do you bring with my green tea, Ari?"

She pressed her bright pink lips together and offered me an apologetic smile. "I'm kind of regretting I brought it up now. I don't suppose I could eat my both words *and* this newspaper?"

"No way. You've officially piqued my interest."
I took the paper from her and didn't even have to
turn the page to be hit square in the face with the
main headline: **Daughter's Battle with
Addiction: Mayor McKinley's War on Drugs
Hits Close to Home.**

"Jesus." I exhaled sharply.

Arianna's sympathetic green eyes bore into me.
"Try not to take it too seriously. You know he's
just pushing a political agenda."

"Yeah. At my expense." I scanned the article,
recognizing the reporter's name as one of my
father's biggest supporters. His loyalty was surely
purchased, and he was a devoted partisan of the
McKinley camp. "God. Did you read this crap?
He comes off as such a caring, devoted father.
And I am made out to be some drug addict that
broke his heart and endangered our family's
strong bond."

I laughed. What else could I do? All of New
York—and the entire country, for that matter—
were reading lies about me spread by my own
father. If I didn't laugh, I'd cry, and I'd already
done too much of that lately.

*It is thanks to the Mayor's devotion and support that
his youngest daughter is now able to lead a healthy,
fulfilling life. Miss McKinley is off to Harvard Law next
semester...*

"My life is a fucking joke." Groaning, I chucked the paper across the room. "The good news is that now the rest of the world knows it, too."

"We all have parental issues. Mind you, the worst mine have ever done was show my ex embarrassing baby photos." She wrinkled her nose. "Sorry. I'm not making this better, am I?"

"It's not your job to make it better." I placed my hand on her arm and gave her a gentle squeeze. "It's my job to live with it, I guess."

My father had threatened that I would regret not participating in his campaign. If this was a warning shot, I hated to think of what was still to come.

"I was in rehab," I said. "The things about my father searching high and low to find the best place for me are lies—he was livid when reports of my stay surfaced—but the stuff about my trouble—"

"Reagan, you don't have to tell me anything."

I nodded. "I know. But as my boss—"

"As your boss I know that you have one hell of an eye for talent. You're also pretty damn good at making heads and tails of all those international contracts," she said. "And as your friend, I really don't give a shit." The tension in my muscles eased as she added, "But if you need anything…"

"Thank you," I said with a warm smile. "I'm doing okay." It was a battle I was still fighting every day, but

AA meetings and private sessions with my new therapist helped. Especially now, when it would've been so easy to go back to being the old Reagan.

"Good. Because, speaking as your boss again, I need you to take contracts over to our next artist later today."

"Oh," I said. *Oh, no.* Dare. "You don't want to do it?"

"I wish, but I have a meeting and this can't wait." She grinned slyly, a mischievous twinkle appearing in her eyes as she winked. I felt my stomach turn. "God, Reagan." She sighed dreamily. "You need to see his paintings to believe them! They're like nothing I've laid eyes on before. The colors, the style, the *subjects*. The ARTIST."

I knew all too well. I lived and breathed Dare's art. Hell, I lived and breathed Dare.

I forced my lips to turn up even though it hurt to keep smiling. Despite our friendship and her obsession with Dare, I hadn't been able to tell Arianna that I knew him. The wound from our last fight was too recent, too raw, and I feared I wouldn't be able to handle all the questions she was bound to have.

"I need you to head over to his studio in Queens this afternoon," she said as she handed me a manila folder. "If we're going to put on this impromptu show, I need these forms signed

ASAP."

Shit.

Two weeks had passed since Dare and I last spoke. Two weeks of me *somehow* holding it together. Mostly by working twice as many hours as I was supposed to, and spending my nights researching the shit out of everything I could possibly think of to find another way to get rid of the threat of Dare's dad.

I'd even called my father again and demanded he throw Daren back in jail. He'd had the audacity to laugh like it was a freaking joke, and said he'd made an offer and if I was willing to take it, I should let him know. Then he hung up on me.

I spent time in the library looking into cases where minors were charged as an accessory to a crime, and what I found wasn't encouraging. Dare could be charged.

After I got home at night, I either helped Rex or went to group meetings, and ignored my parents' calls for family campaign obligations.

I was doing fine—okay, that was a big, fat lie—but at least I wasn't unraveling completely.

The last thing I needed right now was to actually see Dare. It was enough that I had to listen to Arianna gush about him. His unrivaled talent. The allure of his eyes. Things she would like to do to his body. That tortured, brooding artist vibe he exuded. Thanks to her—well, thanks to Dare—I was officially a tortured, brooding curator's assistant.

I'd resisted the temptation to drown myself in the comfortable oblivions I knew pills and alcohol would bring. I constantly fought the itch that was always there, buzzing under my skin, teasing and inciting me on. It was a hell of a battle, but I was doing it. Slowly. Painfully.

Yes, I'd gotten sober for *us*, but I was staying sober for *me*.

Minute by minute. Hour by hour. Day by day.

However, I wasn't sure if I had enough strength to see Dare and walk away. He wasn't just a drug. He was my everything.

He didn't know I was working at the gallery again, so I had a feeling my showing up was not going to be a welcome surprise. God, there was nothing about this that didn't suck.

"You sure you don't want to go?" I asked again, then forced the next words out. "I know how much you enjoyed your last visit."

"It's true." Arianna giggled. "I did. And I wish I could, but I can't miss this meeting."

"Alright, fine." I sighed. "I'll do it."

Even if it fucking killed me.

fourteen
Dare

"Is this okay?" Liz asked for the hundredth time. "Am I okay?"

"Yes," I said. "Just keep still. Everything is great." It was the furthest thing from the truth. The painting was a fucking mess.

In fact, the entire two-hour session had been a pain in the ass.

She kept moving, readjusting her red dress and shifting position in front of the studio's floor-to-ceiling windows, which messed with my continuity and lighting. If this had been a personal project instead of a commissioned job, I would've sent her packing long ago. But Rex had referred the family to me and they were well-paying clients, so I agreed to do a portrait of their twenty-something daughter.

This girl was my hardest subject to date. But that had a lot to do with the fact that I'd been overexerting myself. In the mornings I was working under Rex's guidance, and painting the portrait in the afternoons. My hands were pushed to the limit, constantly aching, but Rex was convinced that the more I used them, the better they would get. And though my style had changed, he believed it was a change for the better. In fact, I'd never seen him so worked up about my stuff before.

Still, I had yet to jump on the bandwagon.

Right now, I was kicking myself for all that time I spent in Amsterdam not painting. Here I was killing myself to paint, desperate to get back to where I was, frustrated as hell that everything hurt and nothing came out the way I wanted, and I couldn't believe I'd wasted so much time.

"How's the picture?" Liz shifted in her seat and smiled brightly. "Does it look pretty? Do *I* look pretty?"

I surveyed the canvas in front of me. Was she beautiful? Sure. Long brown hair, symmetrical facial features, toned body. But everything about her was unremarkable. Uninspiring.

Then again, I'd felt that way about everyone I'd painted since Ree.

Some artists never found their muse. Just like some people never knew true love. Somehow, I'd lucked into both and managed to fuck them up at once.

Being without Ree was like being forced to survive without a vital organ. She was my fucking heart. And now I was on life support again.

By my own doing.

Because of my father.

I needed to get my hands on the bastard. I'd been searching for Stanzi for weeks now and I was no closer than when I started.

"Did you hear what I just said?" The girl was speaking—*again*—drawing my attention back to her face. "Could we take a quick break?" she asked. "I need to freshen up my make-up."

"Again?" The lighting was finally right.

"I feel all shiny and gross."

"It's fine. I can take the shine down." She was pouting now, so I just shrugged. "Sure. Go ahead." What the hell did I care?

As she disappeared into the back of the studio, I made my way to my workbench and swiped my phone off the counter, scanning my missed calls and most recent messages.

No Stanzi.

Fuck.

If I knew where the worm was hiding, I'd dig him out myself. But he'd always been a coward, which was probably the only reason he was still breathing.

I threw my phone down and turned toward the coffee pot, but a movement in the hall caught my attention. Liz had apparently lost her dress in the bathroom and was now in the process of removing her bra.

"What the hell are you doing?"

"I saw the paintings in your back room," she said, slowly peeling off the straps as she continued to walk toward me. "I want you to do one of me. Just like that girl with the long, blonde hair. I want one exactly like that."

My jaw tightened. She'd been snooping, had seen my paintings of Ree. The ones I'd kept from Arianna that were not going to be in the upcoming show. Opening a crate full of images of the girl you loved but couldn't be with was one hell of a kick to the balls, so I did the only sane thing that I could think of and shoved them into the back room.

The last thing I needed right now was a nosy client dropping her underwear. A client whose daddy was paying for a *clothed* portrait.

"You need to put your dress back on," I said. "I'm not going to paint you naked."

She frowned. "Why not?"

"Because that's not what I was hired to do." I shrugged.

"Fine." She stuck out her bottom lip as she stopped in front of me. "Then *I'm* hiring you. Make me look just like her."

You can never be her, I wanted to say. "I'm sorry. I'm not painting nudes at the moment."

"What?" Her gray eyes narrowed. "Wait. Do

you only paint the girls you sleep with?"

"Yeah." I lied.

She arched an eyebrow. "So?"

"*No.*"

Clearly not used to people refusing her, she wove her fingers through the belt loop of my jeans and lowered herself onto her knees, a haughty grin playing across her lips. "I'll pay you double what the blonde paid."

Christ Almighty. What was her idea of currency?

I wrapped my fingers around her wrists and gently tugged her back up. "The *blonde* is my girlfriend," I said. "And if she were here, she'd tell you to put on your fucking dress and go. Now." At this point, I didn't give a shit if I was going to lose the damn paycheck from her father. I just wanted her gone.

Too late. Just as I lifted Liz to her feet, the door of the studio swung wide open.

"Hello?" Ree walked inside, clutching a manila folder to her chest as she surveyed the loft. She froze, her mouth popping open before she quickly pressed her lips together. The pain in her eyes sliced through me like a sharp dagger.

Damn it.

"Oh, shit," Liz said. Recognition flashed across her face as her hands sprang away from my pants. "It's not what it looks like. I swear."

Ree turned to me. "I think it's exactly what it looks like," she said coolly.

I didn't correct her.

I was too pissed that she was standing in my studio. That she'd found out where I lived. That she was deliberately putting herself in danger because she was too fucking stubborn to stay out of it when I told her to.

And from the look on her face, she was just as pissed at me.

Yet even amidst all the chaos and anger, I could feel the hum between us, pulling us together time and time again.

A crazy, stupid love that might not be enough to save us this time around.

fifteen
Reagan

"I'm just going to…" The almost-naked girl crossed her hands over her chest and stood up. "…go get dressed." She ducked her head and scurried off toward the back.

Good riddance. I didn't even bother to look at her, my gaze was locked on Dare's, and there was fire in his eyes.

"Sorry if I interrupted something," I said. "She certainly doesn't have to leave on my account."

"What are you—shit, Ree. You didn't fucking interrupt *anything*. She'd overstayed her welcome."

"But the painting isn't finished." I glanced over at the canvas in the center of the brightly lit space. The model wore a semi-formal dress, her hands neatly folded in her lap, a soft smile on her crimson lips. It was a clean, pretty portrait, though a little safe given Dare's usual style.

"It's a commissioned piece," he said. "Her father's rich and paying me well."

"To take off his daughter's clothes?" I couldn't have softened the edge in my voice if I'd tried. And I didn't bother trying.

The right side of his mouth lifted slightly. "No. She thought of that all by herself." He stared at me intensely. "*Nothing* happened."

"I noticed."

A door opened down the hall and a moment later the girl hurried past without looking at either one of us or saying goodbye.

"Your next sitting with her should be filled with awkward," I said after the door slammed. "Unless, of course, you just pick up where you left off today."

"Come on, Ree. Nothing happened. Nothing was going to happen. There is no one for me but you. There never has been." His eyes bore into mine. "Which is why you shouldn't be here. You shouldn't be anywhere near me until I get this thing over with."

"Or maybe it's exactly why I SHOULD be here. And maybe you should stop being so fucking stubborn and let people help you. You don't have to do everything alone."

"How did you even find—"

"Arianna needs you to sign these for the show." I held up the stack of contracts, pages carefully marked with bright yellow tags, and walked toward him.

"Arianna? You're working for Sabine again?" He nodded slowly. "Of course you are. I should have known." He took the papers from me, then shifted a few bottles of paint to make room for them, his jaw tensing slightly as his fingers wrapped around a black pen. "Un-*fucking*-believable, Ree."

My mind twitched at his words, my ire rising until my eyes followed the flow of his fingers as he signed the papers. My heart broke at the sight of the scars running along the entire length of his right hand and up his wrist.

I gritted my teeth, fighting the urge to reach out and slide my fingers across his paint-speckled skin. Every one of my senses was starved for him no matter how much he was pissing me off at the moment. I breathed in his nearness—he still smelled like paint, so familiar yet so distant at the same time.

He finished signing the last page, paused, then pinned me with his dark gaze, his expression calculating.

"This was *your* doing, wasn't it? The show. You set this up, not Rex." His jaw clenched. As much as I wanted to, I wouldn't lie to him. I nodded once, and he said, "Then I'm out."

"What?! Why? Because it would mean that I'd helped you in some way?" I poked him in the chest hard. "God. It's fine for *you* to help people, but the moment you need help, you've got to do everything on your own. Sometimes you can be such a man, you know that, Dare?"

"I'm trying to keep you SAFE, Ree."

"No, you're trying to keep me OUT." Fuming, I took a step forward and got right in his face. "We're a fucking team. And I will do whatever I can to help you, so just fucking deal with it!"

There was so much tension in the air, I felt as if the entire room was about to combust. Anger and lust fueled a fire that burned between us, scorching our entire world. Dare and I had shared undeniable chemistry since day one, but there was also something even more powerful pulsing between us. Something stronger, deeper, and as terrifying as it was wonderful. Love had the power to both create and destroy. Sometimes in the same moment.

Sometimes in a single kiss.

I couldn't tell which one of us made the first move, but Dare's mouth was suddenly on mine, his tongue parting my lips as he fastened his grip on my hair and pinned me against the edge of the workbench.

His kiss was a dizzying answer to an ache that had resided in both my heart and body for weeks now. Heat flushed my skin and electricity hummed through my veins as my world began to spin out of control. I lost myself in him, moaning his name, running my hands over his back, clutching his t-shirt, fervently tugging his hair.

Dare matched my need with his own, piercing me with his tongue and biting my lips as he dug his hips into me—hard, rough, and wanting. His hands gripped my sides, tightening around my waist in an iron grip. Without breaking our kiss, he lifted me up so that I was sitting on the desk, then slid his hands down my body. I gasped when his palms skated over my thighs to my knees, spreading my legs open so he could wedge himself between them.

"I fucking warned you," he whispered against my lips, his voice so hoarse and severe I felt his words vibrate through me. "Three years ago, I warned you to stay away."

"And three years ago I refused to heed that warning." I pressed my mouth to his, forcing him to experience my words the same way I'd felt his. "Now, I'm even more serious when I say that I'm not going anywhere. I love you too much to run." Sliding my hand over his chiseled jawline, I stroked his lower lip with my thumb. "Your war is my war, Dare. It's your turn to let ME be enough."

"You're not just *enough*, Ree." He kissed the pad of my thumb and shook his head. "You're my fucking everything."

Every cell in my body screamed for him, but I

needed a guarantee. "Then show me. Say we'll do this together and I'm yours. All yours." I cradled his hurt hand in mine, placing his fingers to my lips. "My mouth is yours," I said before guiding him down to my chest. "My heart is yours." Slowly, I took his hand even lower, toward the ache between my legs. "Every part of me belongs to you."

"Ree...*fuck*." He groaned, parting my lips wider, pushing his tongue deeper. His kiss grew even fiercer and more demanding.

It was almost as if he'd been holding back a fragment of himself this entire time—a primal, uncontrolled piece he'd finally chosen to unleash. A greedy part of him that possessed me whole and refused to let go. He fed on me, grinding his hips, inciting my moans to become cries and pleas for more.

More of his lips, more of his hands—so much more of Dare.

But I needed an assurance that we were in this together before I could fully let go. "Say it," I said. "I want to hear the words."

"I love you." His teeth sank into my bottom lip and he sucked it into his mouth, simultaneously biting and licking the tender flesh until I gasped from a mix of pleasure and pain.

"Not those words." I shoved against his chest, forcing him back, breaking our kiss. We were both panting, teetering on the edge. Was it right to demand this from him? No, but I was done living in limbo. If he refused to speak, was I prepared to walk away from us? Hell no, but I would do it nonetheless. "Say it, Dare. Tell me."

A tempestuous storm brewed in his gaze.

"If I agree to let you help, you must promise me something in return." He pushed my hair back, tilting my head up so that his dark stare bore through me. "We're talking about real danger. Fucked up, life-threatening danger normal couples never experience in an entire lifetime together."

"I know," I said. "And I'm not afraid." After all, we'd never been a normal couple. Hell, nothing I experienced with him ever was *normal*. But maybe Dare and I just weren't meant for that kind of life. When was the last time anyone wrote songs or novels about normal, right? "What do you want?"

"Your word that you'll do everything I ask of you." He spoke softly, his expression grave. "My father is an animal. He's unpredictable and callous. If he finds out about you…if I fail to keep you safe…" He gripped my face with both hands and peered into my eyes. "I can't lose you—do you understand?" I nodded, sinking deeper into his touch as he ran his fingers through my hair, sweeping messy strands from my face and gathering them at the back of my head. "Not now, not ever."

"You won't," I said. "As long as you don't shut me out again."

Love was supposed to involve an equal amount of give and take, and be a complete surrender of two souls to each other. As we stared into each other's eyes, something shifted in us both. Something gave way. All the pent up anger and pain I'd felt over the past few weeks spent apart came rushing out of me as a bruising kiss to Dare's lips.

He groaned at the contact, tightening his hold on my hair, as hungry for me as I was for him. His tongue sought out mine, firm and unyielding, leaving me shaking and breathless.

"God, I've missed you so much," he said into my hair, blazing a trail of ecstasy down the side of my face, over my jaw, to my neck, then licking his way back to my mouth.

Without breaking contact, Dare slid his hands to my front and grabbed hold of my blouse, ripping it open, showing no regard for the buttons that clattered to the floor. Before the garment even left my body, his lips were on my breasts, taking turns teasing my nipples through the sheer fabric of my bra as he pushed me farther back on the workbench.

Tubes of paint went flying as he swept his arm across the surface. In the scattered mess, paint oozed out, getting on my hand and side. Dare didn't seem to care. He shoved his materials off to the side, getting even more paint on us in the process as he continued to suck and nip at my breasts. I arched my back and pressed myself into his mouth, begging for more as I writhed beneath him.

"You're so fucking sexy when you moan for me, Ree." He peeled my bra off with his left hand while his right thumb and forefinger worked my nipples into tight peaks. I was quickly losing my mind, pressure building between my legs that was in serious need of release.

Desperate to feel more of his warm skin on mine, I sought out the hem of his shirt and lifted it over his head. My fingers skimmed his perfectly sculpted chest, leaving a trail of cerulean blue as they slowly slid down to his abs. His body was sharper—he looked like he'd lost weight while recovering from his injuries, which just made my heart hurt, thinking about the agony he must've been in. I kissed every single scar that marred his torso, gently caressing the phoenix on his back— the tattoo that hid the deep wound left by yet another one of Daren's dirty attacks.

As I worked my way down Dare's body, his paint-covered hands wound through my hair, dyeing the dark blonde tresses bright, vibrant hues. When my fingers drifted to the waistband of his jeans and traveled farther south, he inhaled sharply and jerked his hips forward, pushing me all the way back onto the desk. The stack of contracts flew off the table, fluttering to the floor.

"Looks like you're going to need new forms," he said, his lips quirking up into a sexy smirk.

I laughed. "Another excuse to see you."

"And another opportunity for me to do this…" He unzipped my pants and slipped his hand down toward the ache that had been starved for his touch. "…and feel this…" A deep moan bloomed deep inside me when he grazed my clit. "…not to mention claim this…" He traced a slow, leisurely circle over the sensitive spot and I nearly came undone right then and there. "…as I make you mine."

"So this is the part where you ask things of me, right?" I panted the words out, teasing.

"No, Ree." The heat in his voice and the gravity of his gaze rocked me to my core. "This is the part where I make you beg for me."

Dare yanked my pants and thong down my legs, knocking off my heels as he tore my clothes off and tossed them behind him. He slid his hands up my thighs, parting them so that I was completely bared to him, and he placed himself firmly between them.

"You're a fucking goddess," he said, leaning over me as his tongue traced my phoenix tattoo.

"Sexy, powerful, and all mine." His teeth scraped along my ribs, then travelled across my chest, clamping down on one erect nipple, causing me to yelp in surprise, then moan in delight. "I hear a lot of moaning and whimpering," he said as he began his descent down my stomach toward my pulsing core, "but not nearly enough begging."

Oh, god. He was going to make me work for it. The thought of prolonging this game drove me to the brink of madness and spurred on my excitement.

I arched my back and desperately offered myself up to his mouth. "*Please*, Dare."

"Please what?" He let out a low growl brimming with impatience, but instead of immediately giving me what I wanted, he took his time exploring my body, painting me with his touch, teasing my skin with his fingers until I was close to tears. "What do you want, Ree?"

My mind spun. What did I want?

"You," I breathed. "Every-*fucking*-where."

Please. Please. Please.

He threaded his fingers through mine and locked my hands against the hard wood beneath me before gently biting into my inner thigh. "Here?"

"Yes." Fuck, yes. But while the sensation made my breath hitch and my hips buck wildly, there was another place I needed him more. "But also…oh, god…" It was hard to think with him sucking on the tender skin. "…more…up. Please, Dare, *higher.*"

"Like this?" He flicked his tongue up my leg, getting closer and closer to exactly where I wanted to feel him. I whimpered as his hot breath skated over my wet folds, but he overshot the target by a mile. His lips touched down on my stomach and I cried out in torturous agony.

Fuck. Me.

I was THIS CLOSE to wrapping my legs around his neck and strangling him. Also possibly being rocked by a spontaneous orgasm. I tried to steady my quivering legs and take control of my arousal, but it was futile to rebel against what I really wanted.

Right now, Dare owned my body—the treacherous thing would only respond to his voice, his touch, his command. The bastard had also claimed my mind, leaving me unable to string together coherent thoughts. Yet, in this moment, I was perfectly happy being imprisoned by him.

"*Dare…*" His name melted on my tongue like dark, sinful chocolate. "Please—*oh, god!*"

He released one of my hands and his fingers clamped down on my nipple as he circled my bellybutton with his tongue. "Say it, Ree. You need to speak up, baby."

No, I needed to *come.*

"Please lick me or I will die." I fisted his dark locks in my shaking fingers and pushed his head lower, waves of excitement surging through my body, settling in my core.

"Well, I did promise to take care of you. And since this is a matter of life and death..." The end of that sentence—and his incredibly hot mouth—ended up buried deep between my legs.

Dare indulged in a long, leisurely lick, the effects of which I felt all the way up my spine. He growled, and I knew the low, carnal sound was a pleased response to how soaked he found me. "I missed you so fucking much. Your sexy body, your sweet taste, your sultry moans." Raising his head slightly, his eyes met mine. "I've been losing my mind without you."

And here I was, losing my mind THANKS to him.

He spread me open with his fingers and ran his tongue along my center, lapping me up then plunging into me. My nails raked over his back, digging into his skin, hanging on for dear life as he worked me into a wild frenzy.

"This is the part where I make you scream my name." He held me down with one hand on my stomach as I writhed beneath the pressure of his unyielding, possessive licks. "Let go, Ree. Let me hear you come." Then he sank two fingers inside me, while claiming my clit with his lips. He sucked me into his mouth, circling his tongue over the nerves, and I completely lost myself in the sensation of being owned by him.

This was the very definition of being wholly *consumed*. Trembling from the pressure. Gasping for air. Tears in my eyes from the immense pleasure. Coming so hard I forgot my own name. After all, there was only room for one word on my lips—*Dare*.

Spasms rippled through me—a visible earthquake in my body—but he kept me pinned to the table, reveling in the tremors and coveting every single drop of my pleasure. When I had nothing left to give, he made his way back up to my lips, kissing me senseless, kicking up my already frantic heartbeat.

"I'm not done with you yet." His delicious promise sent excited shivers over my body. "We're just getting started, baby."

"Good. Now it's your turn to wear my name on your lips." I slid off the table, teetering on the columns of Jell-O that were my legs, using Dare's rock-hard stomach to steady myself. "I want you inside me," I said as I grabbed the waistband of his jeans. I tugged the zipper down, setting him free. It never failed to amaze me that every perfect inch of him was masterfully sculpted. "First in my mouth…" Lowering his jeans to the floor, I slid my palms down the front of his legs and knelt directly in front of him. "...then I want—"

"*Ree...*" His eyes flashed in warning, and my mind was immediately flooded with naughty thoughts of the many things I wanted to do to him. And that I wanted Dare to do to me. "There isn't going to be a *then* if you keep talking like that."

I stroked him with my hand, sliding over his throbbing length as I flicked my tongue over his smooth, hot skin. Licking him once from base to tip, I took him in my mouth slowly, torturously, then deeper and faster, making it my mission to give him just as much pleasure as he'd just given me.

He leaned against the table, gripping its ledge with one hand as his other twined through my hair. "You're playing with fire."

Grinning up at him, I met his eyes and skimmed my fingers over my breasts to my phoenix, down my hip, ending at the spot between my legs. "I'm fucking with dynamite," I said, parting my thighs, touching myself as I licked him. "And I'm looking forward to the explosion that is sure to follow."

Dare cursed and pressed his lips together, his eyes rolling back in his head. His breath was so shallow and labored I couldn't tell if he was panting or groaning. Maybe both. I knew he was close—so close to the edge, so completely lost in me, so fully entwined in us. And I loved that I was the one doing this to him..

Just when I thought he was about to let go, he pulled away and grabbed my shoulders, hoisting me up. He kissed me on the mouth, then grasped my left wrist and spun me around so that my ass was flush against him and my stomach pressed against the edge of the workbench.

"I want to fuse you to me so I can never lose you again." The palm of his other hand glided over my curves, etching his touch into my skin.

"There's nowhere I'd rather be," I said. "Right now. And always."

Dare nudged my legs apart with his foot and bent me over the table, dipping my breasts in the now purplish-brown paint that coated the whole surface. Our bodies were both covered in colors as if we were one of his paintings come to life.

He thrust into me so hard and fast I cried out his name in surprise and ecstasy. With a quick roll of his hips, he drove even deeper, sinking his teeth into my shoulder as he groaned his pleasure. He stayed like that for a moment, completely unmoving, throbbing inside me as I pulsed around him, feeling fuller then I'd ever been before.

Then he was moving inside me, pulling almost all the way out and thrusting back in with deep, long strokes that launched every one of my senses into orbit. The fact that his hands were everywhere only spurred on my uncontainable moans.

He held my waist, hips, and ass, his grip so rough it walked a fine line between pleasure and pain, desire and despair. His other hand slid up my front, over my throat, to my parted lips, his thumb pressing against my mouth. I wrapped my lips around him, sucking to the same rhythm of his thrusts.

Both of us ravenous, insatiable.

He licked his way down my jaw and neck, then back up toward my lips. Plucking his thumb from my mouth, he brought it down under the table and between my legs, rubbing my own saliva over my clit as his tongue met mine in a breathless kiss.

His mouth, fingers, cock—it was too much, too overpowering, too wild. I came so hard my nails left claw marks through the wet paint on the wooden workbench as I screamed his name. Liquid heat spread through me as Dare intensified his pace, panting hard, his own climax chasing mine.

"Goddamn, Ree." His mouth was hot against my ear. "You drive me so wild, baby. Wild at heart, crazy in love, fucked to the bone." With those words, he ground his hips into me one last time, completely letting go, unabashedly filling me with warmth as he collapsed against my back.

"Let's do that again," he said as he kissed my cheek. "I want to watch you as you come. I need to see that pretty mouth scream my name."

"Again?" Turning in his arms, I arched an eyebrow, still riding my post-orgasmic high.

"Again and again." Dare gripped my ass and lifted me up so that my legs wrapped around his waist. "But, first—a shower. Good thing you're already soaked," he teased as I bit down on his bottom lip.

Oh, god.

We were back.

And here to stay.

Finally.

Hopefully.

sixteen
Reagan

"Dare Wilde is an art god!" Arianna said as she opened the front door of the gallery and ushered in two delivery men carrying large canvases. "And he's going to be a filthy rich art god very soon. These babies are going to sell faster than Twinkies at fat camp."

I nodded in agreement, and pointed the uniformed duo toward the back room where we were storing the art until it went up for sale next week. "Dare deserves of every bit of success that's soon to come his way," I said. "He's an incredible artist." And it was way overdue, considering everything he'd been through.

"Dare, huh?" She cocked her head and regarded me. "The way you say his name sounds so…" *Possessive? Protective? Personal?* "…familiar," Arianna said, and I realized it was time to come clean to my new friend.

I twisted my braid between my fingers. "I

haven't been completely honest with you, Ari. Not that I lied...I just left some things out. About Dare." Mostly because I'd been so angry and confused over him pushing me away. "He and I are..." God, we were so much more than just a single word, a simple explanation. "We have a history," I said. "And a present."

As for our future? Now that we were fighting side-by-side...it would be bright.

It had to be.

Though, I had to admit, I'd been on edge lately. Even after what happened between us when I went to deliver his contracts—or, rather, ESPECIALLLY considering that day—all I could think about was Dare's plan and all my dead-end attempts to find some other way to get to his dad. I couldn't bear to see him get hurt.

Again.

Arianna's high-pitched squeal startled me. "You and Dare Wilde?! I can't believe you've been keeping this from me!" She was gaping at me as if I'd grown a second head. "Crap. And here I was, going on and on about him. Practically stalking the guy! I'd been going to his place three times a week under the pretense of business, desperately hoping he'd show me more of his paintings. The special ones Rex says he keeps in his bedroom."

"I have a feeling you weren't there *just* for the paintings." I laughed. Sure, every one of her designer blouses and pencil skirts were the latest fashion, but I'd never seen her wear six-inch stilettos to meet with any other client. There'd also been a few extra undone buttons on her top every time she headed over to Queens.

"Well, I was kind of hoping he'd show me something else while the bed was nearby." She blushed, laughing. "But I guess he was saving *that* for you all along."

"I'm sorry I didn't tell you before," I said with an apologetic smile. "I'm not used to having girlfriends." Since leaving my old world behind, real friends without ulterior motives were an unexpected wonder I was still getting used to. Not to mention, Dare had been going through so much lately that I had no idea how to approach the subject of our relationship with Arianna…or anyone else.

Sneaking around might've been hot in theory, but combined with an actual, viable threat, the gravity of our situation took all the fun out of just about everything. Every time I slipped over to his apartment under the pretense of getting more signatures or checking on new art, I had to look over my shoulder. Every time I kissed him, I had no clue when the next one would come.

Or if there would be a next one.

"You're living with Rex Vogel and you're sleeping with Dare Wilde," Arianna said as she shook her head. "Could I be any more jealous right now?" She smacked my arm good-naturedly, and pointed to one of the canvases. "Let me guess, they've also painted you, right?"

"Only Dare." I bit down on my lip to keep from grinning as my mind went back to the incident on his workbench. Yeah, he'd painted me. In many, many ways. Inside and out. Body and soul. I'd been scrubbing color from my hair for a week.

"Oh, my god!" She clasped her mouth with both hands. "His father!"

"*What?*" A chill shivered over me.

She ran a hand through her dark red locks and shook her head. "This is so embarrassing," she said, groaning. "I kind of told him Dare and I were dating."

"You told Dare's father…WAIT. You SAW Dare's father?!"

She nodded. "God, I'm so sorry, Ree. If I'd known that you two—"

"No, that doesn't matter. It's fine." I waved my hand. "When did you see him? I need to know EXACTLY what happened."

"Umm…" Arianna looked startled by my urgency, but there just wasn't time to explain my freak-out. She pursed her lips and frowned. "Let me think…"

"Did he come here?" I prodded. "To the gallery?"

"Yes. Looking really out of place, actually. Too rough to be one of our regular high-end clients, and way too intense for a hipster on a wine-and-cheese gallery crawl. But let me just say that I now completely understand where Dare gets the tall, dark, and handsome from."

"*Ari.*" I couldn't care less how hot or not the deadbeat asshole was. "What did he want?"

"Nothing much." She shrugged. "Just said that he and Dare hadn't spoken for a while, but that he was trying to make contact again and wanted to meet the people who mattered most to his son. It's kind of sweet if—"

Shit. "Did you tell him where Dare lived?"

Arianna shook her head. "He already knew. Apparently he heard Dare had a girl at La Période Bleue and saw me over at his studio, so he deduced we were an item. And I didn't correct him. I'm sorry." She touched her fingers to her throat nervously. "I guess I was just trying to employ the power of positive thinking. If I told enough people we were a thing, then maybe…"

Double shit. "You told him you were Dare's girlfriend?"

"I'm sorry, Reagan." She bit her lip, suddenly looking panicked. "I had no idea—"

This time, I cursed out loud. "Ari, it's okay. I'm not mad at *you*. Dare's father is a psychopath." Who now probably had a big, fat bulls-eye trained on Arianna.

Fuck. Fuck. FUCK!

Her brows knit together in confusion. "I don't understand. What's—"

"Miss?" One of the burly delivery men walked over to us and handed me his clipboard. "We need you to inspect the canvases and sign off on the delivery."

"I'll do it," Arianna offered.

"No," I said. "It's fine." I took the clipboard and began walking toward the office. "I'll be back in five and then we can go home."

I looked over the paintings quickly, initialed the delivery forms and paid the men. Then I sat at my desk and dialed Dare's number.

He answered on the second ring, his voice filled with warmth. "Ree."

"Dare…" Shit. My hands started shaking as the enormity of the situation hit me.

"Ree? Are you okay?" He sounded so panicked, and I now understood how justified that was.

"I'm fine," I said. "But…there's a problem." I told him what Arianna had said. Every scary bit.

Dare was cursing before I'd even finished. "This is exactly what I was afraid of, why I didn't want you involved." He let out tortured groan. "How did he find out about the show? It's not like he runs in the same circles as your clients. And I specifically told Arianna no advertising."

"You did?" Oh, shit. "Uh…she placed a week long ad in the Times, Dare. I didn't know—" He let out such a string of curses I had to hold the phone away from my ear for a moment. I could feel his anger vibrating through it. "Dare, she didn't mean to—"

"No," he said. "She didn't mean to alert my father, but she didn't fucking listen to me. FUCK." He ranted for another minute, then said, "He is NOT getting his hands on you. I will kill that bastard if he even tries."

I didn't doubt Dare's ability to protect me even for a second. But who the hell was watching out for him in all of this? Had he forgotten *he* was in danger, too?

"We're closing now," I said. "I'll make sure Arianna is off safely, and then I'll head back home. I know we're not supposed to see each other, but—"

"To hell with that." He practically growled. "From now on, I'm not letting you out of my sight."

"So you'll meet me later tonight?" I needed to see him, touch him, hold him.

"No," he said. "I'm coming to get you right now. I was chasing another lead on Stanzi, but came up empty-handed. Again. I'm on my way back into the city right now. Don't leave the gallery. I'll be there in twenty."

"I can get to Rex's by myself," I said.

"I'm already on my way."

"Dare, it's—"

"You can't drop this on me and then expect me not to worry. I'm on my way." Okay, he had a point. I was about to hang up when he said, "And Ree?"

"Yeah?"

"I love you," he said, his voice softening slightly. "You know that, right?"

"I know." I felt it with my whole heart. Warmth flooded my body at his words, easing away some of the fear coursing through me.

We'd figure this out. Together.

"You're mine to take care of and protect," he added before hanging up.

Arianna called my name from the front, so I placed my phone back in the pocket of my dress pants and locked up the office.

"This was left outside when I went to take in the dog water bowl." She was turning over a small package in her hands. "We didn't have any other deliveries scheduled, right?"

"Nope. Dare's stuff was it for today. Maybe the guys forgot something?" I crossed to the front door, propped it open, and stepped outside. The crisp fall air felt good in my lungs after being inside all day.

"I guess it's possible, but what kind of artwork

fits into such a small box?" Arianna called from inside.

"I have no idea," I said, as I glanced around the street. "Dare doesn't have any pint-size paintings."

At the mention of Dare's name a guy across the street who'd been looking inside the gallery suddenly shifted his gaze to me. The hairs on my arms stood on end.

Something was wrong.

Every cell in my body was screaming *Danger!*

I turned to look at Arianna holding the little box, starting to rip through the paper, and whipped my head around to see the strange man turn the corner at a dead run and disappear out of sight.

No. It couldn't be. Dare's dad wouldn't stoop to—

"Arianna!" I screamed. "STOP!"

She glanced up at me in surprise as she pulled open the flaps.

"PUT IT DOWN!" I lunged for the door. "THROW IT!"

Time froze. I screamed a soundless scream.

And then the entire world exploded.

seventeen
Dare

Rushing to the Mount Sinai emergency department, not knowing whether Ree was dead or alive, ripped my world apart. Over the past couple of months, I'd had my body beaten and broken in countless places, my mind and spirit crushed, but none of it compared to this level of pain and panic.

When I'd gotten to SoHo, I couldn't even get close to the gallery. Fire trucks, ambulances, and cop cars were everywhere, flashing red and blue lights for blocks. I'd parked, jumped off my bike, and sprinted to Ree's street, where bright yellow caution tape and several officers blocked it off.

Smoke billowed out through the shattered windows of the building where Ree should have been waiting for me. If I hadn't forced her to stay at the gallery—thinking she'd be safer there, foolishly believing I could protect her—she would've been halfway to Rex's by now.

Instead, I'd signed her fucking death warrant.

Oh, god.

Don't let it be true…don't let it be true!

People all around me were talking. *Someone had been killed*, they'd said. *It had to be terrorists. But why would they blow up an art gallery?*

They wouldn't. But my dad would.

I tailed an ambulance all the way to the hospital, hoping Ree was inside. I abandoned my bike at the nearest lot, and was now racing toward the ER.

Praying for the best. Fearing the worst.

She was here, thank the gods, but they wouldn't let me see her. Two hours of pure, hellish agony passed before anyone even answered a single question. Despite lying about being her brother, they refused to tell me anything, threatening to have me removed if I kept harassing the nursing staff for information. Ree's actual family—the ones who could probably bypass all the red tape—were nowhere in sight.

A uniformed officer walked in through the ambulance entrance, and spoke quietly to the triage nurse. She pointed to me and I felt all the blood inside my body rush straight to my head. My ears were ringing, my hearing going in and out, and I was only able to make out half of the words he was saying.

A homemade bomb. Not terrorism, but a

targeted attack. Couldn't reveal any more right now, but did I have any idea who could've wanted to hurt my sister?

"Yes. Daren Wilde." I heard myself tell him from a million miles away. *Find Daren fucking Wilde.*

"Can you come down to the station to leave a statement?" the cop said. "Doesn't have to be today. But tomorrow or the next day. It'll help."

I nodded—hell, I'd agree to almost anything if someone would just let me see Ree—but I knew better than to believe the police would actually be able to do anything about it.

"Is she…" I said, the pressure inside me reaching an unbearable high. "…okay?"

The cop rubbed his jaw, tensing slightly. "I think it's best if you speak with the doctors."

And that was when I lost it. Unable to contain myself any longer, I stormed into the patient area, shouting for Ree.

A nurse was on me in an instant, but I shook her off.

"I *have* to see her." I growled the words out.

"Everyone has people they need to see here." She tried to turn me around and push me toward the waiting room again. "We will come to get you when you're allowed back here." She pointed toward the doors, sounding like a drill sergeant. "Out! Now!"

But I sidestepped her and strode past a few rooms. "REE!"

The nurse was out of breath when she caught up to me. "Sir, I'm going to have to call security if you don't settle down."

"I have to see her! PLEASE! I have to know she's alright!"

"Dare?" A small voice floated from the room to my right.

Her voice.

The moment I ran inside and pulled back the curtain, my knees buckled. Ree was sitting on a gurney, cut, bruised, and bandaged, but alive. My entire world shook, then rushed into focus as the realization that I still had her hit me. Colors became brighter and sharper. Sounds louder. My heart beat a wild rhythm as tears of joy sprang into my eyes.

"SIR!" The nurse charged in after me. "You cannot just barge in—"

"No, please," Ree said, holding up a hand as if to stop her. "Please let him stay. I want him with me."

The nurse glared at me, harrumphed, mumbled her assent, then left in a huff.

Then I was at Ree's side, wrapping my arms around her, fighting the urge to crush her to me. I couldn't remember the last time I cried. I'd vowed never to cry again when I was seven years old because it gave my father too much joy. But seeing Ree, touching her, feeling her warm breath on my neck, I couldn't hold back the tears.

"Oh, god, baby…" I brushed the hair out of her face and peered into her watery eyes. "I thought…I—"

She crushed her soft lips to mine with so much painful need my heart clenched. My Ree. My other half. I kissed her back harder than I'd intended, giving her everything I had, knowing just how close she'd come to being stolen away from me.

When we pulled apart, I took my time examining her, gently running my fingers through her hair, over her face and arms, careful to avoid all bandaged areas.

"It kills me to see you hurt," I whispered hoarsely. "If I'd been more careful, if I'd made you stay away…" I shook my head and groaned, kissing her again. "But I couldn't. I fucking couldn't. I gave in to my weakness. *You*."

"Stop blaming yourself, Dare," she said tearfully. "Loving you might be beyond my control, but being with you is my choice." Cupping my face with one hand, she drew my head down so our foreheads met. "You were my very last thought when the bomb went off."

"God, Ree…" I kissed my way down her nose to her lips. "I came so fucking close to losing you."

"They told me I was lucky because I was outside," she said. "The blast knocked me out, and aside from a concussion and twenty stitches here"—she lifted her bandaged forearm—"most of the cuts are superficial." Her words were muffled by my shirt as she rested her face on my shoulder. "Arianna was the one holding the package…but they won't tell me if she's okay. Oh, my god—" She pulled away, her eyes suddenly wild. "I have to know, because…"

Her voice faltered as I started to shake my head. "At the scene they said someone had been killed…and I didn't know if it was you or…"

"NO!" She was waving her arms in front of her as if the gesture could somehow erase what I'd said. "No, no, no!" She collapsed into my arms, sobbing. "She wasn't supposed to die! She was holding a package meant for me!"

"I'm so sorry." There was nothing else I could say. I felt as just as shitty, maybe even worse because all of this was entirely my fault.

Ree looked up at me, her face a mixture of shock and pain. "Arianna was just laughing and teasing me about you," she said in a hoarse whisper. Horror and anguish entwined around her words. "She was going places, Dare. She was going so many places. She can't be gone! Not like this!" Tears streamed down her cheeks, sobs rocked her body. "I didn't get to her in time! If I'd been faster…"

Then you'd be dead, too.

I thought the words, but I couldn't bring myself to say them out loud. Instead, I just pulled her closer and let her cry.

"My father is going to pay for this," I said into her hair. "I swear to you, Ree." Nothing could undo the damage he'd already done. Nothing could bring Arianna back or erase Ree's scars. But I would make sure the asshole went down for his sins.

In the meantime, I wasn't going to let her out of my sight. I would chain myself to her if I had to. Take a bullet for her. Die for her.

We stayed locked together for what felt like an eternity. Ree sobbing as I tried to soothe her and keep myself from losing it, too. After a while, she stilled and her breathing became more even.

"Reagan!" The voice startled us both. Letting go of her, I turned in the direction it had come, bristling at the sight of the tall, blond guy crowding the doorway.

"Archer," Ree said, a sad smile lifting her lips.

Asshole, I thought.

"Holy shit, baby girl. I saw the news." In a few strides, he was beside us. "I recognized the gallery and called a friend at the NYPD to get the details. What the hell happened? Are you okay?"

Ree looked up at me, then shook her head. "My friend," she said, tears welling up again. "She was killed."

"Shit." Archer reached out and grasped her hand. "But you're okay?"

Him touching her irked me, but I relaxed slightly when I saw the concern in his eyes. He might've been on my shit list, but the preppy prick seemed to genuinely care about her. And Ree needed more people who gave a damn.

But that didn't mean that I was going to stand there and let him keep touching her.

"She's far from okay," I said, forcing his attention to me. "But she's alive."

Archer let go of her hand, considered me for a moment, then shifted his stance so that he was facing me. "Look, man," he said, extending a hand. "I'm sorry for the crap that went down in Paris. I was a dick. And I nearly lost one of my best friends over it. I'm willing to make peace if it means keeping Reagan happy."

I looked at his hand, then reached out and grasped it. Not that I'd admit it to anyone, but I was vaguely impressed that he apologized. Still, a sickening feeling settled in the pit of my stomach as I thought about how much easier Ree's life would've been if she'd just said "yes" to Abercrombie, here. For starters, no one would be trying to *kill* her.

wild at heart   159

Archer grinned at me before turning to Ree. "Your dad is outside speaking with the police and the press."

Of course the bastard would cover his tracks first before checking on his daughter.

Ree's gaze widened and met mine, her lips parting as she said, "I have to get out of here, Dare. They want to keep me overnight for observation, but I can't stay. I can't stay another minute. Not with Arianna…" Fresh tears welled up in her eyes. "And not with him coming here."

I could understand that. "I'll get your stuff," I said, then nodded to Archer. "Find someone to start the discharge papers."

His eyes darted between Ree and me, and he pressed his lips together into a thin line, looking like he was about to tell us this was a bad idea—*no shit.*

"Okay," he said, to my surprise. "Consider it done."

"Thank you," I said as Ree let out a small sigh of relief.

Ten minutes later, she was fully dressed and had signed the last form while Archer left to bring his car around. The surly nurse from earlier seemed even more pissed at me now, but I didn't care. Ree needed to be away from her dad in order to deal with the death of her friend, and I was going to make sure she got at least that little bit of peace.

We slipped out of the hospital and had almost made it to Archer's car unnoticed.

Almost.

"Oh, dear. Reagan!" Her mother's high heels clicked along the pavement as she ran up to us. "What are you doing outside? I was just speaking with the staff and arranging to have you transferred to a private room." She extended her hand as if she was gesturing to a small child. "Come on, now. I'll call Doctor Montgomery and make sure you have the best care while you heal. They said you have stitches on your arm." Her perfectly arched brows flew upwards. "We have to make sure it doesn't scar."

Was this bitch for real?

Ree shook her head. "No. I'm going home with Dare and Archer."

I placed my hand on the small of Ree's back to steer her away as her father approached, but he clasped my arm with a hard grip.

"Enough games, Reagan," he said, more to me than her. "You need to come with us."

"No," Ree and I both said at the same time.

"I am not letting you go off with this common criminal." He practically spat. "This man has a record five miles long. If you knew even half the things he's been involved in…"

"We both know you're the one with the highest

body count here, Mayor." I gritted my teeth, seething. "You let my father out of prison and started something you have no control over. Don't you realize *he* did this?"

"A juvenile delinquent's word goes far these days, does it?"

Goddamn it. My fingers twitched; I wanted to punch him so badly, but that would only give him an excuse to arrest me. So, instead, I took a deep breath and said, "I'm not letting Ree leave with you or anyone else."

"She needs to be with her family right now," her mother said.

"I am." Ree looked at up me and smiled. "I'm with the only person who has ever loved me."

"Two," Archer said, coming around the other side of her, and standing with us. "The only two who've ever truly loved her." Then he lifted his arm toward his car. "Now, let's get you two home."

As we drove away, the last thing I saw was the dead-hard glare of the mayor.

Good fucking riddance.

eighteen
Reagan

I didn't remember the drive home. My head pounded, my body ached, and my mind slammed the doors on reality, taking me far away from this moment in time. The sounds of traffic faded out and were replaced by the echo of Arianna's laughter, her friendly chatter, her plans for the future.

A future she'd never have.

Because of me.

Because of my father.

I wished I could escape to another time, a different place.

Anywhere but here.

Anywhere but the present.

My life might've been fucked up before, but today's events had taken things to a whole new level.

I barely registered Archer pulling up and parking outside of Rex's. The next time the world came into focus, he was speaking to Dare, his eyes sad, his voice laced with concern.

"Call me if she needs anything," he said. "Anything at all."

Dare nodded and shook Archer's outstretched hand. "Thank you."

Death had a way of throwing people together and making allies from adversaries.

Before I could even blink, Archer was getting back in his car, but something in me panicked. Nothing felt safe. No one I cared about was safe. What if something happened to Archer on his way home?

I hurried over to his Porsche and knocked on the window.

"Please don't go," I said. "Can't you come in, just for a while?" Then I glanced up at Dare, begging him with my eyes to understand that I wasn't ready to let anyone I loved out of my sight yet.

Archer's eyes went to Dare, and he started to shake his head. "I don't think I should…"

But then Dare pressed one hand against my lower back, put the other on the passenger door, leaned down and said, "No, you should. Stick around. If Ree wants you here, I want you here."

When Dare stood back up, I leaned into him, my throat closing, my eyes overflowing again.

"It's okay, baby," he whispered into my hair.

"Come on, let's all go inside."

Before we could even turn around, Rex burst through the front door. "WHAT ON GOD'S GREEN EARTH HAPPENED? I've been watching the news, worrying my ass off, and neither one of you had your phone on!"

Dare filled him in as we filed into the house. Rex led us into his living room, where I curled up in my favorite spot on the couch with Dare by my side. Rex went back into the kitchen to put on water for tea while Archer sank into an armchair across from us, his expression concerned and confused.

"So, what's really going on?" he asked, leaning back and stretching his long legs out in front of him. "Because SOMETHING obviously is." My eyes met Dare's. "Look, I'm here to help if you need it." Archer nodded at me. "You know I'd do anything for you, Reagan."

He would, I knew that. And after everything he'd already done for Dare and me, I knew we could trust him. I glanced at Dare again, a silent question on my face, and he shrugged.

"What the hell," he said. "He's already heard half of it."

So I told Archer everything.

Every. Little. Thing.

"*Holy shit.*" He'd drawn his legs back, and was leaning forward, his elbows on his knees, his eyes huge.

Rex had caught the tail-end as he'd come back in with a cup of tea for me, then sat down next to Dare.

"Have you gone to the police?" Archer said, his voice rising. "Have you told them your father is responsible for the explosion, Dare? Because THAT's enough, right there, to put him away."

"They know." Dare put his head in his hands. "They won't find him. Not unless he fucks up…and my father never fucks up."

"Well, you can't just sit around waiting for him to blow something else up…" I could tell by the strain in his voice that Archer was getting agitated. "Do you want to go somewhere? I can book you both on a flight today." He started scrolling on his phone. "Where do you want to go?"

"I'm not going anywhere," Dare said. "And I'm not fucking waiting around anymore." There was something in his voice that made my panic level skyrocket. "I'm done. I've hit dead-end after dead-end looking for Stanzi, so I'm just going to have to confront my father without any actual proof and hope he bites."

"*What?!*" Rex and I said at the same time.

"No!" I shouted, sitting up and gripping Dare's knee. "You can't. Your father will ki—" I choked on the word, tears springing to my eyes in an instant at the mere thought. "I just lost Arianna. I cannot lose you, too. You can't do this."

"And I can't just sit around and wait for him to strike again," he said, his eyes glittering with anger and desperation. "That could have been YOU tonight. I can't—" His jaw clenched and he wrapped his arms around me, his voice tight with emotion when he spoke again. "He'll kill you if he gets another chance. Tonight proves that. I've got to do something, Ree."

"But there has to be a better way," Rex said. "There has to be something else."

"There's nothing else, Rex. I've exhausted all my sources. This is the only thing I've got on him." Dare's shoulders sagged.

"Okay, so even if that's true, you can't go to Daren with nothing. He'll see right through you, and you know it. He's a mean son of a bitch, but he's also a smart bastard. You think it's a coincidence you can't find any trace of Stanzi? It's because someone doesn't want you to."

Something was prodding and nagging at the back of my mind. Something my father had said tonight. *If you knew even half the things he's been involved in...*

"But what if it isn't?" I said to Dare.

"What?"

"What if it isn't the only thing you've got on him? What if you've blocked stuff out? Because there was a lot more that he did, right? And you were just a kid." Dare contemplated my words, then nodded. "Maybe we can get him on something else, something that won't send you to jail, too."

"Yeah, but—"

"I know someone who has a file on you that is *five miles long.*" Anger coursed through my body the more I thought about my father and his hand in all of this. His snooping. His dirty dealings. He was to blame for everything. "If we got hold of that file, then maybe you'd see something in there that we could use instead. Something that doesn't require Stanzi's proof. It's possible, right?"

The gears were turning in Dare's mind, and he nodded. "I guess it's possible, but I don't think—"

"Then just give me a couple of days, okay? Before you do anything suicidal like go after your father, give me enough time to get into my father's office and see what I can find."

"He's hosting a party tomorrow night," Archer said. "Schmoozing New York's finest."

I got to my feet and started pacing in front of the couch.

"Perfect," I said, then stopped in front of him. "Are you going?" He nodded. "Can you keep my father busy for a while to give me time to get the files?"

"It would be my pleasure."

Dare was shaking his head again. "What if you don't find anything? Or what if there's nothing in there that helps us?"

I stared at Dare, my heart thundering at the thought of him in his dad's hands again. I didn't know what to say because I wasn't willing to ever let him follow through with his plan.

"Then we go after him together," Rex said quietly. "You can't do this on your own no matter what. We've already seen what happens when you try."

"I'm going to be prepared this time. I wasn't—"

"*No*," Rex said, his tone stern. "You're going to go with help this time, son. With *me*. And there are people I can call to back me up."

My eyes watered again as I knelt in front of Dare. "Please, Dare. Please just give us a chance. Do it for me."

He reached out and gently cupped my face, his thumb brushing a tear from my cheek. And then he nodded. "For you."

I breathed out in relief, pressing deeper into his palm.

I hadn't been able to save Arianna, but I had one last chance to save Dare.

I just hoped I wouldn't let him down. Because there was no back-up plan after this.

nineteen
Reagan

"Reagan!" My father's voice boomed across the hallway, echoing off the woodwork, and making me freeze. Fuck. I'd thought he was in the drawing room with the Trumans, Fitzgeralds, Huntington-Chases, and all his other rich cronies, getting them to empty their wallets all in the name of his political gain. And the favors they'd eventually receive, of course.

The whole thing made me sick.

"Oh, my poor daughter!" he said as he walked toward me, his arms outstretched in the perfect imitation of a loving father. What a crock of shit. "I am so glad to have you home where you belong."

I'd been thanking my lucky stars all the way over here that Archer had mentioned this party. After all, I couldn't exactly show up here during the day and riffle through my father's desk with my mother and the house staff lurking about.

This was the perfect opportunity. Or so it had seemed until my father spotted me and decided to make this a photo op for his campaign.

When he got close enough to me, he saw the look in my eye and knew I was not about to play along. So he ushered me into his office, making excuses to anyone who would listen.

"She's just not ready to talk about it yet," "Such a traumatic experience," and "The poor thing is feeling overwhelmed by it all."

God, the man was the master at deception. He was the Houdini of the political world.

Once he'd closed the door, he dropped the sappy act, crossed over to his desk and pulled a cigar out of the drawer. As he clipped off the end, he said, "To what do I owe the pleasure? I assume you didn't come here for the cocktails or the witty conversation."

"There's nothing witty about swindling people out of their money."

"I am not swindling people, Reagan." He laughed out loud. "They're practically begging me to take it."

"They scratch your back, you'll scratch theirs."

"That's how the world works."

"And what do you get for releasing a criminal from prison?" I said. "How is Daren Wilde scratching your back?"

He smiled, flashing perfectly white teeth. "You

came back, didn't you?"

I gaped at him for a moment. "Was it your plan to also get me killed? Because he tried to blow me up yesterday, unless you missed that." My voice got tight as I added, "But he got Arianna instead. Was THAT a part of your deal, too?"

My father slammed his hand down on the desk, the sound reverberating around the room. "And that never would have happened if you'd come home and left that filthy artist alone. If you had done what you were *supposed* to do." My father's eyes hardened and his lips thinned. "I don't understand why you can't just be a team player, Reagan. I've given you everything you've ever wanted."

"No," I said, feeling the heavy burden of his disappointment mix with my own exhaustion. More than anything, I wished things weren't like this between us. "You gave me everything *you* wanted. And you took a lot away."

"How dare you, after all I've done for you?" His face reddened, and he unbuttoned his suit coat, flinging it open. "You know, I didn't want it to come to this, but you have secrets which, if they came out, would ruin your reputation. I would hate to have to take that tactic with my own flesh and blood, but you are pushing every one of my buttons, Reagan."

My mouth dropped open and I felt the blood

drain from my face. The fact that he would try to throw that in my face was almost too much. Almost. Except it was a classic McKinley move.

I narrowed my eyes at him. "Go for it. After what happened last night, I couldn't care less. Besides, that secret will end up hurting you more than it will me because I'll tell them the whole story."

He slowly shook his head, for a brief instant looking almost sad. "You don't even *know* the whole story."

"What's that supposed to mean?"

"Nothing," he said, the word clipped, curt. "Mark my words though, Reagan. You do not want the truth coming out any more than I do." He turned and looked at me. "But I will do it if I have to. And I have a whole team of PR people to spin the story the exact way I want. You, my dear, do not. Remember that." He stood up and took a puff of his cigar. "So do make sure that you are smiling when you rejoin the party."

There was a quick knock on the door. It opened and Archer stuck his head in.

Oh, sweet heavens, thank god.

"Mayor?" he said, an eyebrow lifted as he quirked his thumb toward the party. "They're asking for you out here."

"Thank you, Archer. Reagan and I are finished here, anyway." Without another word or even a glance my way, my father swung around his desk, crossed the room and disappeared through the door.

Archer tilted his head toward the way my dad had gone and winked. I mouthed a *Thank you* to him and he grinned before shutting the door.

I was finally alone in my father's office—alone with the weight of his disappointment and the guilt of Arianna's death hanging about me. The room was thick with secrets, of a world where large sums crossed this desk regularly.

With Archer's promise to keep him busy until he received my text, and given how very pissed he'd been when he left, I was willing to bet all of my father's money that he wouldn't be coming back anytime soon.

I didn't have many friends, but I certainly had the right ones.

I looked around the office and sighed. This was a long shot and somewhat crazy move, but I had to try. He had to have a file SOMEWHERE dedicated to every bit of dirt he'd dug up, and this was my only chance at getting it.

Maybe this time, in this particular instance, it would turn out advantageous to be a McKinley.

I slipped around his desk and started opening drawers. They were full of files, but I didn't see Dare's name anywhere. Or mine.

I tried to open the last large drawer, scraping my

stitches across the arm of the chair, and cursed out loud. Dammit, it was locked. The file was probably in there. Even though I knew it was futile, I opened the middle drawer and searched quickly, but found no keys. Of course not. That would have been too easy.

I slammed the drawer shut, sat back in his chair, blew the hair out of my face as I stared at his black computer screen.

His computer.

Jesus. Of course. God, I was such an amateur.

Turning it on, I glanced at the door, praying that Archer would be as good as his word. My father's desktop came up and I did a quick search for files containing Dare's name.

Eight came up. Great. But I couldn't read through them right now. I'd need to—

Shit. A memory stick.

I opened the top drawer, but there were none in sight.

Oh, my god. Why didn't think to bring a memory stick? Arianna would think this was so—

No. I couldn't think about Ari right now. I swallowed hard. I had to stay focused.

Okay. I would email them to myself. But the browser wouldn't connect, and when I glanced down at the little internet icon, I could see why. Of course. Why would I expect there to be an internet connection when I really needed it?

Across the room was my father's printer. Plan C. That would have to do. I hit print on each file, looking back and forth between the door, the printer, and the computer screen.

I did a quick search for Dare's father's name as well and landed a couple of files. I hit print on those, too. I was about to search my name, when the door handle started to turn. The printer was still going—I couldn't help that—but I quickly closed all the files as the door opened.

And my blood froze.

The printer went blessedly silent, with a stack of sheets waiting for me to pick up on the other side of the room, but I couldn't take my eyes off the person leering at me from the doorway.

"Reagan," Jackson said, stepped into the room…and closed the door behind him.

My heart flew out of my chest when I heard it click shut.

No. I did not have time for this.

I clicked the shutdown button and watched the computer screen flicker off in my peripheral vision, never moving my eyes away from Jack. No matter how much I didn't want it to, my breathing became rapid and shallow—as if my body remembered to be frightened even when my mind was fighting mad—and I leaned forward in the chair, ready to spring out of it if I needed to.

"It's been too long," he said as he leaned against

the door looking like he had no intention of going anywhere for a while. "What a wonderful surprise to see you here. I'd thought it was going to be a stuffy, boring night, and then you blow in like a pretty summer breeze. The party got infinitely better when you arrived."

"Fuck off."

"Ah, now. That's no way to talk to the son of your father's most influential political colleague." He strolled into the center of the room, brushed his blond hair out of his eyes, and smiled at me. "What say we take our little party of two somewhere else?"

He reached the opposite side of the desk, and I turned off the monitor with a shaking hand, then warily stood up.

There was a desk between us. He couldn't reach me. And there was a penthouse full of people. They would hear me if I screamed, right?

And I would scream my head off if he even touched me. I would scream before he even got close.

"Not now," I said. "Not ever." I glanced over at the printer again, the light flashing on and off, and took a step toward it. "I have enough to worry about right now—I can't deal with you, too. Go away. Leave me the fuck alone."

Jack stepped in my direction.

"Come on, Reagan. We had such a good time

together before, didn't we?"

I grabbed a heavy paperweight from the desk, ready to hurl it at his head if he took another step toward me. "You're talking about out in the Hamptons, right?" Jack nodded, his twisted face lighting up at the mention. "You fucking raped me, you asshole—"

"Reagan." Pierce stood in the now open doorway, an unsure expression on his face. "I was asked to come find you." He looked hard at Jack. "Everything okay in here?"

Jack shrugged, and I rounded the other end of the desk, scooped up the papers from the printer, and was at Pierce's side in seconds, stuffing the printed files into my bag. I swallowed hard, wondering how much of that Pierce had heard— half caring, half not-giving-a-shit—and slid out of the room behind him.

"Pierce?" I said when he didn't turn around to follow me out.

"You go ahead, Reagan," Pierce said. "Jackson and I need to have a little chat."

I rushed down the hall, my heart pounding, not even looking behind me to see Pierce close the door. I shoved the papers farther down into my bag, and zipped it shut. Pushing past guests, I kept my head down and shot straight for the elevator, feeling like I couldn't get out of there fast enough.

A cork popped in the ballroom, and I flinched, my heart jackhammering against my ribcage.

All around me people were laughing and talking, drinking and toasting each other, and all I could think was *How could they?*

How could they be so happy and carefree when Arianna lay cold and dead in the morgue? How could they pretend that bad things didn't happen to the completely innocent? How could they not see that dangers lurked everywhere, waiting to hurt the people you loved?

I felt like my entire world had changed in one night. In one fatal blast.

Turning, I pressed the call button for the elevator, my eyes starting to water, sobs trying to claw their way out as my mind filled with thoughts of Ari again. But I would not make a scene here. I would not give my father more headlines to help with his campaign—Mayor's Daughter Collapses in Grief at Fundraiser. I had no doubt he'd be out here in a nanosecond, ready to throw his arms around me for the accompanying photograph.

I shook my head, feeling more strongly than ever that I did not belong with these people, and that sometimes family—the true meaning of family—was who you chose to invite into your life, rather than who you grew up with.

Pierce's voice suddenly echoed down the hall,

and I turned to see Jack following him out of the room, his gaze landing on me and staying glued there.

I pressed the button again. Why wasn't the damn thing here yet?

"Reagan!" My mother rushed out of the ballroom. She planted herself in between me and the elevator. "You cannot leave so early." Panic flooded her face as her eyes darted to the guests. "You haven't even shown your face yet. What are people going to think?"

I didn't fucking care what anyone thought. Not anymore.

"Tell them I wasn't feeling well," I said, then glanced at my sister's disapproving expression as she watched me from across the hall. "Or, what the hell, why don't you tell them the truth? Tell them the guy my father let out of prison a few months ago tried to blow me up yesterday, and ended up killing my friend."

Then the elevator doors opened and I slipped inside, reaching around for the button to the ground floor before I'd even gotten all the way in.

The last thing I saw as the doors closed, besides the shocked expression on my mother's face, was Jackson turning to smirk at me before he headed down the stairs toward the lobby.

Exactly where I was going.

twenty
Dare

"Wait, hold up, Ree. Slow down." I pressed my phone to one ear and put my palm against the other to block out the sound of traffic going by. "Did you say someone's following you?"

"Yes." She was breathing hard. "He's about block behind me. I don't know where to go."

Fuck. I knew I shouldn't have left her there alone. I tossed my coffee in the trash, bolted out of the shop and threw a leg over my bike. "Where are you?"

"Fifth Ave, near the bottom of the Park." Her voice shook, which sent my pulse hammering. If my father or one of his thugs laid even one finger on her…

"You know the south entrance to the park? Sixth Ave?"

"Yeah."

"I'll meet you there in a few minutes. Just keep walking, okay?" She didn't say anything, and for a moment I panicked. "REE? Are you still there?"

"Yeah. Just hurry, Dare. He's freaking me out."

"I'm on my way."

The motorcycle roared to life and I wove my way through traffic and turned onto Sixth Avenue. Several blocks up, I could see the entrance to the Park, and sped toward it as fast as I could. At 58th Street I had to stop for the light and I scanned the sidewalks, looking for her long, honey-colored hair.

I spotted her hurrying toward the corner a block away, looking for me, then glancing behind her. And that was when I saw him. Tall, blond, and menacing. He strode up behind her, grabbed her by the arm—the one with twenty fucking stitches in it—and pulled her into him.

And I saw red.

The light turned green and I floored it around the taxis and sedans, aiming for the sidewalk where Ree struggled with her assailant. I didn't even think about it as I rode onto the sidewalk, flew off my bike, and ripped the guy off of her.

I pulled her behind me and dove for him, knocking him backwards several feet.

"What the FUCK do you think you're doing?" I came at him again, punching him square in the jaw, ready to beat him to a pulp if I had to. Fuck, I WANTED to do it, and it was taking all my control to keep myself in check. Blood roared in my ears, and I couldn't feel anything but raw, primal anger. I grabbed the lapels of his jacket, yanked him forward, and rammed my forehead against his. "You touch her again, I'll fucking kill you. You understand me, asshole?"

The guy glanced over my shoulder at Ree and smirked. I grabbed his face with my bad hand and squeezed, which hurt like fuck, but no way in hell was I letting go.

"You want to see if I'll really do it?" I squeezed a little harder and pain flickered into his eyes. I brought my face close to his. "*Try me.*"

His eyes met mine and he smirked again.

And that was all it took.

I let go of his face, pulled back, and hit him again. He yelped in pain, holding his hand to his nose as blood gushed out of it. My hand was throbbing like a son-of-a-bitch, but the guy staggered backwards. Then he cursed, pivoted on his heel, and sprinted back down the block.

"Don't you dare come near her again!" I yelled at his retreating back. "I won't let you live next time."

When I turned around, Ree was watching me wide-eyed, her whole body rocked by tremors. I was at her side instantly, pulling her into my arms, kissing the top of her head.

"You okay?" I said, leaning back just a little so I could see her. "Did he hurt you?"

She shook her head. "I'm okay."

I cupped her face in my hands. "I'm so sorry I wasn't there. I never should have left. I should have just waited outside until you were done."

"No, I left early, never even pretended to go to the party as I'd planned because I got into my father's office right away. And I wouldn't have wanted you stuck outside waiting for hours. It wasn't supposed to go like this."

"With my father it rarely goes the way you'd expect," I said.

Her eyebrows shot up. "Your father?"

"That guy was probably one of his thugs. A plant, judging by his clothes. Looks like my dad knows about you for real this time." I pulled her closer again. Fuck it all. I couldn't lose her. If my father did anything to her, there would be no saving him from me.

Because I would have nothing left to lose. The bastard probably didn't factor THAT in when he'd decided to ruin my life. I would rip him limb from limb, and I'd enjoy every little bit of it.

"Dare?" Ree said quietly, hesitantly, like she wasn't sure she wanted to tell me. "That wasn't one of your dad's thugs."

I scanned the sidewalk where the prick had been moments ago, then I looked back at her, confused.

"How do you know?"

She bit her lip, shaking her head slightly.

"Because I know him."

"What? Who the fuck was that?"

Fear filled her eyes, which nearly sent my heart into overdrive. She was scared of that guy. No doubt about it.

"Ree? Who was it? Does he work for your dad? Is your dad threatening you again?" I ran my hand up and down her arm. "It's okay, baby," I said. "I'm here."

"No, he's not..." Her eyebrows slanted up toward the middle of her forehead, and her breaths came out short and choppy. "That was...that was Jackson."

The world around me went silent, and for a moment all I could hear was her voice echoing in my head. *That was Jackson. That was Jackson. That was Jackson.* Before I even realized my feet were moving, I was already storming down the block after the bastard, fueled by pure hatred and fury.

I'd find him and I'd kill him. Right here, right now.

"Dare!" Ree's voice pierced the red-hot rage of my consciousness. "Stop!" Her hands wrapped around my arm and tugged. I looked down at her, out of breath and frightened, and came to a halt. "You can't hurt him, Dare. He's Senator Fitzgerald's son."

"I don't care who the fuck he is. He's not getting away with it."

"He already did." She shrugged sadly. "And we have bigger things to worry about right now. Let's just go home, okay?"

She was right. We had more pressing worries, but standing there staring down the street where that monster had disappeared, I swore he would pay for what he did all those years ago. If I ever got my hands on him again, he would pay dearly.

Ree brushed her thumb across my cheek. Her touch was featherlight and warm, instantly easing my anger. I couldn't help but melt in her hands, and I marveled that she had this effect on me. No one in my life ever had. But then I'd never loved anyone like I loved Ree. Spending these last months apart had nearly killed me.

"Jackson won't ever hurt you again," I promised her. "I won't let him. You're safe." She nodded, her eyes watering. "You're mine, Ree. And when this is all over, I want you to be mine forever."

The remnants of my rage numbed every other feeling in my body on the ride home, and it was only after I'd parked the bike and we'd gone inside that I realized how badly my hand hurt. I winced when I handed a glass of water to Ree.

"Oh my god, your hand." She gasped, reached out for it, then pulled back. "I'll get you some ice."

She slid the papers off her lap and hurried into the kitchen. I sat down on the couch, and picked up the printouts, scanning them. Detailed notes about all the crimes I'd committed over the years, every dirty deed I'd ever been involved in and even some that I hadn't. My entire sordid past was laid out in front of me. Looking over the files, I seemed like a real low-life.

There were even pages on my dad.

Ree returned with an ice pack, placed it on my hand, then sat down next to me, drawing her legs up under her as she picked up some of the papers.

"What's all this?" I said.

"Files from my father's computer." She looked a little sheepish, waving the paper around. "This was the only way I could get them."

"You did well," I said. "It's all here." My heart clenched at the thought of her reading through my dark, horrible history, because once she finished, she'd know all of my secrets.

Every sinful one.

And she'd probably want nothing more to do with me.

"Ree." I tried to pull the pages out of her hands. "Why don't I look through them?"

Her brow crinkled. "I can help. I'm actually ridiculously smart, you know. Pre-law at Columbia, summa cum laude."

"Yeah, but—"

"Dare," she said, and her tone made me stop. "I love you." She waved the papers again. "This is *history*. This is who you *were*—in large part because of your father, I know that. It's not who you *are*. I love who you are, and that's not going to change. Regardless of what I read." She leaned over and kissed me, her lips melting against mine. "So just calm the fuck down already."

I kissed the smile that came with those words, then sucked her bottom lip into my mouth. She moaned as I deepened our kiss, ran one hand through her hair, and wove her tresses through my fingers.

But then she suddenly pushed me away. "No way. You're not distracting me from this. No matter how amazing you kiss. THIS is more important." She scooted down the couch from me, and settled in with a stack. "You need to make us some coffee while I go get Rex, because this could be a long night. There's a lot to go through."

I raised an eyebrow at her. "*You* are going to drink coffee?"

"For you, Dare," she said, "I'd do anything. Now let me read."

Six hours later we'd combed through every page at least three times, and had come up with nothing.

No-*fucking*-thing.

And no Stanzi.

Fuck.

"You know what I don't get?" Ree said, fingering the pages, a thoughtful expression on her face.

"What?" At this point, I was no longer getting ANYTHING. I was so fucking tired, my eyes were about to fall out of my head. Rex had passed out an hour ago, and was softly snoring in the old, beat-up, green recliner.

"Stanzi. There's no mention of anyone named Stanzi in all of this stuff." She ran her thumb across the papers like it was a flip-book. "Everyone else you've ever dealt with in any capacity is documented in detail, right?"

I nodded. "As far as I can recall. And there are some here that I don't remember."

"So where's Stanzi?"

"Maybe your father missed one. Though the thoroughness of his files makes that hard to believe." The mayor's work on my background was alarming. It appeared nothing was truly as secret as you thought.

Ree was already shaking her head. "My father doesn't miss anything. No...it's almost like all info on Stanzi is *purposefully* missing."

That didn't make any sense. But it was almost four o'clock in the morning, and we were both exhausted—a lot wasn't making sense.

"But why would your father leave something as important as Stanzi, and his connection to the Douglas case, out of the files?"

"So no one who went digging would find it." Ree's eyes gleamed as she stood up and started pacing the room, her mind clearly going a million miles an hour. "Remember when Rex said that someone didn't want Stanzi to be found?" She froze, her eyes as huge as bright blue saucers. "*Oh my god.*"

"What?"

"Holy shit, Dare. This is HUGE." She sank down to her knees and stared at the pages spread all over the coffee table.

"What is? Ree, tell me."

"HE KNOWS." Her gaze locked on mine.

"What?"

"My father. He knows about Stanzi." Her voice was low, filled with horrified amazement.

"But why would that…oh, shit." It hit me all at once. If her father knew about Stanzi, it meant he was withholding information about a cop's murder.

Which made him a guilty party, too.

Holy. Fucking. Shit.

We had the bastard.

And, willing or not, he was going to help us bring my father to justice.

twenty-one
Reagan

The ride up in the elevator felt like it took an eternity. For once in my life I couldn't get to my parents' apartment fast enough.

My father had started this and he was going to end it.

Today.

Dare and I hadn't slept at all—we were both too worked up, too anxious to get to my father first thing. So two hours later, with Rex still sleeping in my living room, here we were.

The doors opened to an empty foyer. Taking a deep breath, I laced my fingers through Dare's and stepped out. The white walls seemed even more colorless with Dare by my side, and I felt embarrassed to have him witness this mausoleum of a home. There was no warmth here, nothing inviting.

We paused for a moment as he took the place in.

"I just can't quite picture you here," he said.

"That's because I never fit in." I tried to see the place through his eyes. "I was always a stranger in my own home." I tilted my head to the right. "Come on. He'll be in the dining room."

We walked down the pristine hall, the shiny floor spotless, our footsteps making the only sounds in the whole place. It had never felt so quiet here.

Never felt so on the verge of a life-changing moment.

My hands started to shake. Facing my father with what we knew felt earth-shattering in immensity.

Dare gave me a little squeeze. "It's okay, Ree. I'm here with you." His quiet voice bounced off the walls, carrying down the length of the hall.

About halfway down, I turned and led Dare into a room on the left. My father sat at one end of a long table, his coffee cup on its way to his mouth when he looked up at us from the Times. His eyes flicked from me to Dare, and his expression darkened.

"I can only assume you are here to apologize for your behavior last night, Reagan," he said, setting his cup down and leaning back in his chair. "And I have no idea why you brought *this*—" He waved his hand at Dare. "—with you."

"This," I said, "is Dare."

"I know." He crossed his arms over his chest. "I am waiting, Reagan."

"Then you're going to be waiting for a long time. I didn't come here to apologize. I came here to tell you that you are going to put a stop to this. Today."

"Now, Reagan, you already know my terms."

I pressed my lips together, and nodded once. "I do. But there's something you forgot to factor in." I held his gaze in silence for a moment. "Stanzi."

My father's face blanched, surprise flashing in his eyes for a brief moment before he recovered his bravado. With false calm, he raised his eyebrows. "Stanzi? I have no idea what—"

"We *know* that you know," I said. "And for this one we have proof." A lie, but he didn't know that. The omission of Stanzi in his files was not evidence that would hold up in any court. I only hoped he would assume I'd gotten hold of some information. My father wrote down EVERYTHING. There would be a file…somewhere.

His face had turned to stone, and I'd never seen so much anger in his eyes. But he didn't say anything. Neither confirming nor denying my accusation.

It was the lack of denial that meant we had him.

"Accessory to murder, if this gets out. Of an

undercover cop, at that." I let go of Dare's hand, pulled out a chair, and sat down, never taking my eyes off of my father's face. "You stop this now. You supply Stanzi's whereabouts to the police in an anonymous tip, he gives Daren up for murder. You ensure Dare is either kept out of it or granted total immunity, and that his dad will never see freedom again between this and the murder of Arianna Saxon."

"*Who?*" My father said it like she was nobody, his eyebrows knitting together.

"The woman who died in the gallery explosion." My throat felt thick. "Who died in my place." I swallowed hard, and glared at him. "And if you know where Daren is, you give them that, too." It felt surreal to be talking to my father like this, to finally have the upper hand.

He didn't speak for the longest time, and I thought we might've lost him. But then he took a deep breath, exhaled slowly, and said, "Anything else?" His voice sounded rough, raw.

"You accept Dare," I said.

"You have no idea all of the things he has done. Reagan, he's—"

"I have *every* idea, Dad. I know all of it." I pulled Dare over to me, gripped his hand tightly. "This man is not the person in your files. That's not who he is anymore. This man is an incredible artist, a kind, caring, generous, and loyal person.

He's amazing, and I love him. He's my heart."
Dare's other hand squeezed my shoulder. "You
accept Dare AND you ban Jackson Fitzgerald
from every aspect of your life. I don't ever want
to see him again." I leaned forward, my eyes
boring into his. "You fucking *owe* me that after
everything you did."

He started shaking his head. "You're asking for
a lot—"

"That's the deal. Take it or lose your political
career, and likely your freedom, too."

My father pointed at Dare. "He would lose his
as well, if this came out. He would face the same
charges. Are you willing to risk his freedom, too?"

"Fuck, yes," Dare said, and pulled out his
phone. "Should we call right now?"

Searching my face, my father said, "He would
go to prison for a very long time."

"Maybe he would," I said. "Maybe he wouldn't.
He was a minor at the time and under the
influence of his father. A good lawyer would
argue that he could not be held responsible. It's
likely he would walk." I paused for a moment to
let that sink in. "The same cannot be said for
you."

My father's shoulders sagged, the fight gone out
of him. "Fine. I'll take care of everything."

"Today," I said. "This morning."

"Yes." He nodded. Then he looked at me, a

mixture of respect and disappointment coloring his expression. "You would have made a damn fine lawyer, Reagan. You are wasting your true talent."

"She's going to make a damn fine gallery owner," Dare said as he pulled me to my feet and pressed his lips to my forehead. "Her talents are limitless, and there is no waste when you're doing what makes you happy."

I held tight to Dare the whole way home, my arms around his chest, my front pressed against his back. I'd thrown my arms around his neck and grinned like a maniac once we were in the elevator, but it wasn't until he parked the motorcycle outside his apartment and we'd gotten off that I crowed.

Literally. And loudly. On the street in Queens at seven o'clock in the morning.

"Shut the fuck up!" Someone yelled from a nearby window, and Dare and I grinned at each other as he grabbed my hand and we stumbled through his door. He scooped me up into his arms and kissed me hard, until I was breathless.

"You were AMAZING," he said.

"Oh my god. Did you see his face? I have never seen my dad beaten by anyone." I gazed up at him in wonder. "I can't believe we did it. But we DID

IT."

"*You* did it." Dare laughed.

"WE did it." I kissed him again. "Two parts, one whole."

Victory was sweet. This high—of winning, of defeating his father AND mine—it felt so huge I was sure it would never wear off.

We'd beaten them both in one move. Check-fucking-mate.

"I just wish…" No, I was wrong. It was wearing off fast.

He cupped my face between his hands, searching my eyes. "What, baby?"

"I just wish we'd won a little sooner. Arianna…" And I couldn't stop the tears this time. I was wracked with guilt, my chest heaving, my entire body shaking as the wound of her death opened anew.

"I know." Dare pulled me into him, smoothing my hair. "Me, too." He was quiet for a moment, then said, "Move in here, Ree. Today. You and me, we'll make a new start together."

I nodded into his shirt. "I don't want to ever let you go again. I'll go pack up my stuff at Rex's and bring it over this morning. You want to come?" I held him tighter. "I'm not quite ready to let you out of my sight."

He groaned and squeezed his eyes shut. "Oh shit, I can't. I'm supposed to be heading downtown to the police station. They called yesterday. They want my statement. I have to leave now if I'm going to make it." He pressed his forehead to mine and inhaled. "But I can do it another day if you want?"

I did want.

But I shook my head. "No. You should go. Get it over with. Bring Ari's killer to justice."

"Why don't you head over to Rex's now," he said, "and I'll meet you there and help you pack and carry things back here when I'm done?"

"Sure." I hated the idea of him going someplace without me right now, but there really was no good reason to keep him here. It was over. The danger had passed. "I suppose I should let Rex know as soon as possible anyway. He still needs help setting up his stuff."

"We'll both help," Dare said. "We're not abandoning him, you're just moving a few blocks away." He tipped my chin up to kiss me again. "And tonight," he said, "I think we should talk about the future."

"As in…?"

"As in us. Together. Committed." Love filled his eyes. His hands slid down to my stomach and rested there. "Maybe some other future things, too."

Oh, my god. Was Dare actually hinting at what I thought? Wow. Sometimes life made you realize just what was important, and helped you sort out what you really wanted.

And I wanted a life with Dare.

I smiled up at him as his fingers traced my lips. "You have the most beautiful smile in the world," he said.

"You put it there. You have filled my life with beauty, Dare Wilde. In every possible way." I pulled him into a hug one more time even though I knew he needed to get going. It was just so hard to let go…after everything.

"You want a ride over to Rex's?" He leaned his chin on top of my head, relaxed his arms around me.

I shook my head. "I'll walk."

I sank into his embrace, feeling like everything was finally going to be okay. It wasn't perfect, but it would be soon. After everything we'd gone through, things had to get better.

Because, really, how could they get any worse?

twenty-two
Reagan

As I set Rex up in his studio like I always did, I recounted everything that had happened that morning. I expected him to rejoice about our win, but he was very reserved.

"I'll relax when Daren is safely off the streets," Rex said, sitting down on the stool in front of his easel. "I'm sure your father will do what he's promised, but it's not over until that bastard is put away." He pointed at me. "You still need to be careful. As does Dare. Don't celebrate your victory until you actually have it in hand. Or behind bars, in this case."

Wrapping my arms around Rex, I gave him a kiss on the cheek. "Thank you for everything, Rex," I said. "You've been my guardian angel through all this, and I love you for that." Taking a last glance at his setup to make sure he had everything he needed, I started toward the stairs. "I'm going to go pack up my stuff. If you need anything, just shout."

"Ree, I'm serious." His brow furrowed. "I've known Daren a very long time. He won't go down without a fight."

"And I know my dad," I said. "Things are already in motion. This is going to be over before you know it." It had to be. There was no more room for pain in our lives. From now on, we'd be free to enjoy every moment of the happiness that awaited us.

I slowly climbed the stairs, running my hand on the banister, feeling like I was saying goodbye to my home. Opening the door, I paused for a moment to take in the space. Dare had lived here seven years ago. Wow. I'd never thought about the fact that when Dare had been getting his life together, mine had just started to unravel.

Seven years later, here I was in the exact same place, seeing my life finally come together as well. I didn't know if it was Rex or this space, but I was grateful all the same.

I couldn't help picturing Dare at eighteen, determined and maybe a little scared, and I wondered if we'd met back then, if our lives would have turned out differently. Would we have fallen just as hard for each other?

A big part of me believed Dare and I were meant to be—always had been, always would be—so even if our paths had crossed at another time, we would have undoubtedly recognized something within each other, would have been drawn into each other's fire.

We would have discovered that we were two parts of one whole.

It felt wrong to be happy in the shadow of Arianna's death, but I knew in my heart that she would have been happy for me. Knowing that made me feel like it was okay for me to both mourn the end of her life and celebrate the start of mine.

There were no more strings attached. No families tearing me away from Dare.

A new beginning. A new life. A brighter future.

I stuffed my clothes into my bags, and packed up my laptop and books. As I was stripping the sheets off the bed, I thought I heard Rex shout.

I paused, my head tilted toward the door, catching some mumblings. I knew it had to be Dare. It had only been an hour since he'd left— he must have finished quickly, probably just as anxious as I was about being apart.

God, I was so glad he was back already. I planned to spend the next day, week—hell— YEAR glued to his side. I'd work on my career. He'd paint. And then there was that thing he'd said about...other things. Maybe I could finally have it all. I'd fought hard enough, hadn't I?

I gathered the sheets and towels to throw them

in the washer in the basement, and started down the stairs, but halted when I heard the voices.

"I don't know where he is," Rex said, his voice strained as if he was in pain. "And I have no idea what girl you're talking about. As far as I know Dare doesn't have a girlfriend. You know him, Daren. He's just like you—one is never enough." Rex tried to laugh, but it came out sounding more like a cough.

Holy fucking shit. I froze on the stairs, my arms full of bedding, completely unsure what to do. Maybe I could get back upstairs and call the police. I lifted my left foot and placed in on the step behind me, praying it wouldn't make a sound. Then I slowly lifted myself up one stair. As I was about to do it again, Rex cried out in pain.

"See, the problem here, Rex, is that he's become a little too much like *you*." The man's voice was hard and gravelly, like he'd spent a couple of lifetimes smoking ten packs a day. "He's MY son, not YOURS, you hippie fuck. I made him a man, and you've undone all my hard work. I should fucking kill you for that right now."

Scuffling sounds and a muffled cry sent my heart thundering against my chest. I had no idea what to do. I knew Dare's dad was dangerous— deathly so—but I couldn't just stay here and listen to him hurting Rex.

Fuck. Fuck. Fuck!

I shifted the bedding under one arm, pulled out my phone, and dialed 911 as quickly as I could.

"Let's try this one more time, you fucking art fag. Tell me where I can find my fucking son and his fucking girlfriend, or I'll cut off your fucking hand."

"Daren, please," Rex said, his voice filled with fear. "You and I go way back, you know I'd tell you if I knew anything at all. I respect you, Daren. I always have."

"You're fucking afraid of me, old man. As well you should be. Eddie, hold him down."

My feet were flying down the stairs before my mind had time to even contemplate what I was about to do.

"NO!" I yelled. "Leave him alone." I threw the linens onto the floor and waved my phone in the air. "The cops are already on their way," I said, trying hard to keep my voice steady. "If you leave now we'll just tell them it was a false alarm." I glanced at Rex, who they'd pinned to the floor, one guy kneeling on his injured arm. He was looking at me with such fear I had a hard time staying in place. "Won't we Rex?"

Someone hit my hand from behind, sending my phone flying across the room. It slid on the floor and came to a stop at the feet of one of the men. He lifted up a black-booted foot and crushed it. My eyes grew wide as I realized who he was.

An older, rougher, well-worn version of Dare.

"Who the fuck are you?" He was a couple of inches taller than Dare, had the same dark hair and dark eyes. There was no mistaking him—I could have picked Daren Wilde out of a line-up, sight unseen.

"I'm—" Shit. Rex was shaking his head at me.

A guy nudged Daren and pointed, and I could feel the blood draining out of my head as recognition washed over me like the ice cold touch of Death. He'd been the one on the street outside of the gallery. He'd seen me, heard me talking about Dare.

He knew who I was.

NO, NO, NO!

"That's her," the guy said. "That's his girl. The one I saw on the street at that gallery."

Daren's mouth lifted into a cruel smile as his eyes slowly took me in from the top of my head all the way to the floor, and then back up again.

"RUN, REE!" Rex yelled.

Arms closed around me from behind as Daren whipped around and stomped on Rex's hand. Leaning over him, he drew his gun and pointed it at Rex's stomach.

"You lied to me, you fucking son of a bitch. You know what happens to liars?" He tilted his head to one side as if he was waiting for Rex to respond. He wasn't. "They die. A slow and painful death."

Then he pulled the trigger.

I was screaming and clawing at the arms around me as the guy was pulling me toward the door.

"NOOOO! REX! NOOOO!"

The other men had released Rex. His hands immediately went to his abdomen where blood quickly soaked his white shirt, a horrifying scarlet circle spreading out around him. He looked up at me, shock so clear on his face, and mouthed the word *No* over and over again.

Thrashing my head, I kicked and screamed, struggling to get out of the guy's arms, but he held fast. I had to get to Rex. I had to call for help. They were all walking away from him, leaving him lying there in an ever-growing pool of his own blood.

"NOO—" A heavy hand slapped my face, cutting off my scream, sending stars into my vision.

"That's enough out of you," Daren said, then nodded at the guy holding me. "Go put her in the car. If she gives you any trouble, just fucking hit her again." Then he looked me in the eye and smirked. "Welcome to hell, Princess."

Reagan and Dare's epic saga comes to a climax and conclusion in...

untamed

episode 5: rebel roused

Untamed 5: Rebel Roused

With a ring in his pocket, and the future on his mind, Dare Wilde comes home to discover that his worst nightmare has come true. Ree's been taken, his best friend shot, and his father is still on the loose.

He thought he'd won. He thought everyone he cared about most in the world was finally safe. But his life has never been that easy.

Now it's a race against time—and his monstrous father—to save the ones he loves most. Can he help Rex and rescue Ree? Will he even survive another encounter with his father?

Ree and Dare's story comes to a close in this final book of their saga. But will the end be a happily-ever-after or an epic tragedy?

AVAILABLE NOW

All books in the series now available

Want to be emailed when Jen and Victoria release a new book?

Get on the Mailing List!

Enter your email address at either Jen's site (www.jmeyersbooks.com/the-list) or Victoria's (victoriagreenauthor.blogspot.ca), and you'll be the first to hear when new books are available. Your address will never be shared and you'll only get emailed when a book has been released or is newly available.

acknowledgements

We've got major love for our editor, Stevan Knapp. He has the sharpest eyes around, and is a big reason this book is so shiny inside.

We've also been blessed to have some serious cheerleaders on our side, spreading the word, supporting us, grumping at our evil cliffhanger endings (but being ever so forgiving about them, too.) So we'd like to give extra special thanks to TeriLyn, Amanda, Jolene, Jena, Nicole, Beth, Helen, Justin, Catherine, Kristyn, Diana, Pam, Meli, and Taryn. You all rock! (We probably missed someone because we've been overwhelmed with our readers' generosity and enthusiasm…so if we missed you it was completely unintentional. We love you, too.)

And lastly, we thank *you* for reading our books. You're the reason we write.